CANDLELIGHT REGENCY SPECIAL

CANDLELIGHT ROMANCES

The Lady Rothschild

SAMANTHA LESTER

A CANDLELIGHT REGENCY SPECIAL

Published by
Dell Publishing Co., Inc.
1 Dag Hammarskjold Plaza
New York, New York 10017

ISBN: 0-440-15495-2

Printed in the United States of America
First printing—September 1978

*To May and Bud Cowan,
friends.*

CHAPTER ONE

Penelope Rothschild sighed in disgust and laid aside the needlepoint with which she'd been struggling. Muttering an oath unsuitable to any lady of the times, she got to her feet and smoothed the simple dress she wore over her slender, boyish figure. For a long moment she stood thus, her eyes on the discarded needlepoint, her thoughts on the women of London who had so little to occupy themselves that they daily took needle in hand for such idiocy.

"Beg pardon, m'lady," Becky, the ever-indulgent abigail, said from the doorway, "the earl would have you present in the library." The servant's glance went to the needlepoint and an amused expression of resignation crossed her features. "The needlepoint progressing ill, ma'am?"

Penelope smiled wryly. "How anyone can sit for hours with such as that is beyond me, Becky. Better it were if my brothers were again able to take me on the hunt with them. Did my father say what it was he wished of me?"

"No, m'lady. Though it was only this morning he gave such orders as are necessary for the giving of a grand party."

Penelope's eyes brightened. "A party? That's marvelous. It's been so long since there has been any such thing in these halls. I'll go right away." Sweeping past the abigail, she called over her shoulder, "Do what you will with the needlepoint, Becky." Then she was out of the chamber and away.

Lord Rothschild, Earl of Donley, smiled fondly as his daughter rushed into the room. Her breathing was heavy, he thought—unbecoming a lady of her standing. She was, however, his only daughter and, as usual, he would mention nothing of her constant desire to go from one site to another with the utmost haste.

"Father, Becky has said you wish to see me. Is something amiss?" she asked, curtsying nicely before him.

He paused a moment, seeing much of the girl's mother in her. The smile that touched his eyes spoke of a love not forgotten and still mourned. Finally, when her questioning eyes had raised to meet his, he spoke. "There will be a party in Rothschild Halls on Friday. You should prepare yourself to act the part of a lady."

The delight registered in her brown eyes warmed his heart.

"And, Father, might I ask the reason for such a surprise as this?"

"Indeed you may. It seems only proper to afford your brother Charles such a pleasure for his homecoming."

"Charles?" She breathed the name of her youngest brother. "Charles is to return from the colonies?"

"No longer colonies, my Penelope. Now the United something or other. But, yes, he is to arrive on the twelfth. Does that please you?"

"Oh, yes, Father," she bubbled, going to him and placing a kiss upon his cheek. "It pleases me beyond words. But he was of such good cheer in his letters. What reason has he for his return?"

The earl's features darkened. His glance fell from

her face, then lifted again. "Your brother does not choose to return. It is of necessity that he does so. It is naught for you to concern yourself with, however. It is a man's business."

"And a Rothschild's, I take it," she argued. "Am I not a Rothschild, Father?"

The impertinence of the statement reminded him again of his casual raising of this girl who, had her wishes been granted, would have been of another gender. "You are indeed a Rothschild, my Penelope," he answered finally. "But there are those happenings which concern men. This is one of them."

"You are saying Charles has been stricken," she exclaimed, her eyes widening in fear. "Oh, Father, what is it?"

A sigh of defeat left his lips. It seemed nothing would do but that he tell the girl the truth. "In truth, my girl, nothing has befallen your brother. Rather it is . . ."

"Yes, Father?"

"Very well, you prying wench, I'll tell you, else I will know no peace in my own household. Your brother returns because of a note I included with his last dole."

"A note, Father?"

He nodded. "A note informing him that the family Rothschild is in such financial straits that it would be impossible to remit his dole in the future." His head dropped until his chin was touching his chest. "It is unbelievable that the Rothschilds should be found in such a condition."

Penelope was silent for a long moment. Then, her eyes filled with pity for this father she loved so well, she asked, "The investments of Mama and yourself, Father. Surely . . ."

"The investments are gone, child. The lands are, for all purposes, the property of he who holds the paper on them. Rothschild is without funds."

"But how, Father? Why?"

He shrugged miserably. Refusing to meet her eyes, he muttered, "An old fool's antics at the gaming tables, my child. A feeling of certainty that the next roll of the bones would return that which was lost."

Tears filled the eyes of the girl. She dropped to a sitting position at her father's feet, her head on his silken-clad knee. "Oh, Father, how awful for you."

His hand came out to touch the softness of her auburn hair. For a moment, tears to match hers threatened his vision. "For me, child?" he asked. "How like you to say such a thing. But I don't think your brothers will be of the same vein with their declarations."

Her head came up, exposing the silvery paths of tears across her cheeks. "Rob and Monty too?"

He nodded. "I've sent them word this very morning. They will, of necessity, be of good advice to arrange for the security of their families."

"Even their lands, then? Everything? Ah, Father, the cruelty of it all for such to strike the head of the Rothschilds."

"Your brothers will, I am sure, be vexed that such a thing has happened. It was something akin to pestilence which drove me beyond common sense at the tables."

"But the party, Father? The expense? What . . ."

" 'Twill be the final such thing, I fear," he answered. "But such a one that befits the return of a Rothschild from a foreign country."

"Oh, Father, what are we to do?"

"I go to speak to the baron when your brothers have made their feelings known. Perchance there will be a method whereby he will allow the Rothschilds time for repayment of the debts."

"The baron?" she asked, pulling away from him to get to her feet. "Is it Baron Von Lentin of whom you speak, Father? That fat old Prussian pig who features himself such a mark of society?"

He nodded shortly. "It is. However, my girl, you must show respect for the baron. He is, after all, nobility."

"Hah!" she snorted in an extremely unladylike manner. "He is a pig." Her eyes narrowed. "Is it to him you have lost the Rothschild fortunes, Father?"

The eyes of the girl were on him. There was no damning in them for the man who sat as if waiting for the whip to fall, only a questioning that demanded an answer.

"It is he," the earl answered with a nod. "He is one of those who are close friends with Lady Luck. With her on his arm, there was little problem for him to relieve an old fool of his wealth."

"He cheated," she exclaimed. "He cheated you, Father. He must have."

His jawline became rigid at her outburst. "Enough of that. A man of his position would have little reason for cheating. It is abhorrent that you should even think such a thing, much less give voice to it. I will hear no more of this."

Aware of the anger in the man, she dropped her glance. "Yes, Father. I only meant—"

"It is man's concern. I told you that. It is naught of yours. Your brothers will be here momentarily, so go wipe the tears from your face and make yourself presentable."

Nodding, she turned and quickly left the room, wiping at the tears which cascaded down her cheeks from overflowing eyelids. Once in her room, she studied herself in the glass and made the necessary repairs to her person. A mental picture of Charles, youngest but for her of the Rothschild children, entered her mind and suddenly she smiled. "He'll know what is to be done," she decided aloud, as if asking the mirror to agree.

* * *

It was just short of an hour later when Becky came to announce that the older brothers had arrived at the halls and to inform Penelope that the earl wished her presence immediately. With a word to the girl about picking up the room, she left and made her way once again to the library.

"Ah, Pen," her brother Robroy exclaimed as she entered the room. "Were it not for the hair and the attire, you'd be taken for a lad. How are you?" He extended his hands in welcome, and she came forward to place a peck of a kiss on his cheek.

"And the love of your life, Rob," she asked in jest, "is she still bosom heavy to the point of imbalance?"

"Still the same Pen," the eldest of the Rothschild children said, handing her over to Montgomery, the second in the family line. "Do something about the wench, Monty, else she'll have me turning her upend for correction."

Monty accepted her kiss of welcome with only a slight smile breaking his face. Then, with a nod of acknowledgment to her, he turned to the earl. "Well, Father, your message spoke of an urgent matter to be discussed by the Rothschilds. Shall we get on with it?"

The earl met the coal-black eyes of his second son and nodded. "Indeed we shall. It concerns two things. First, your brother will return from across the sea on the twelfth. We shall have a gala to welcome him on the fourteenth."

"Splendid," Rob exclaimed. "Has he then made his fortune or given up the attempt?"

"Neither," said his father. "He comes at my demand and request. He returns because I no longer shall send him his dole."

The two brothers exchanged curious glances. "Something concerning his actions in the colonies has displeased you, Father?" Rob asked.

"Nay, nothing."

"Then why deprive the poor lad of that which is rightfully his? It would seem to me—"

"It matters not what things seem," the earl interrupted. "What matters is the fact that the Rothschilds can no longer afford such an outlay."

"You jest, Father," Montgomery said, his voice colored by the hint of uncertainty. "Why, Charles has an income of—"

"Nothing!" the earl snapped. "Nor does either of you. If you'll allow me, I'll explain my words. Sit. Please."

When all of them were seated, the earl cleared his throat and, as if the second telling were easier, explained the going of the Rothschild fortune. When he'd finished, his two sons sat in disbelief for a long moment. Then Montgomery, his face filling with color, jumped to his feet. "You lost everything at the tables, Father? Everything? How *could* you be so stupid? How could you—"

"Mind your tongue," the earl snarled. "It is not a lackey you assault with your tone."

"But well it might be," Rob exclaimed, anger apparent in his eyes and bearing. "Were you mad, Father, to gamble with that which did not belong to you? To put us all to ruin for your own pleasure?"

The earl's eyes clouded under the lashing. He dropped his glance from theirs and hung his head. Then he saw his daughter rise to her feet.

"I cannot believe my ears," Penelope said, "that these two brothers of mine should carry on so toward their own father." She fixed Rob with an angry glance. "You, Rob, have you forgotten that father is the head of the Rothschilds? How could he be amiss, as you suggest? Are not all Rothschild funds his to do with as he will?" She swung her burning glance to Montgomery. "And you, Monty. How could you show so little respect for the man who raised you?"

"Control your tongue, lass," Robroy snapped. "This

is not for the likes of you to be parcel of. Go to your quarters and employ yourself with something woman-like."

"Go bite one of your famous steeds, brother dear," she snarled back at him. "I will not stand by and allow the two of you to use our father in such a manner." Turning to the earl, she said softly, "Father, come. Let us retire from the presence of these two dolts who believe the Lord blessed them and no other." She reached a hand to touch the shoulder of the old man.

His hand came up to cover hers and his head lifted. His lips were set in a grim line when he spoke. "I accept the responsibility for what has befallen us. In truth, it is your promised fortunes which are lost. I can make no excuse. However, until your brother Charles arrives, I have no intention of discussing the matter further. I called you here to give you notice that your families must search for some new source of dole. I repeat, the Rothschilds are without finances."

He got to his feet and, with Penelope's hand on his arm, left the library. Behind him, two unhappy heirs stood in silent contemplation of their new status.

CHAPTER TWO

Charles Rothschild clutched the side rail grimly as the ship tossed its way toward England. With only one day more of this fighting of a rampaging sea, he feared that he might yet miss seeing his beloved England again. Beside him, standing as if on a different deck entirely, was a man six feet in height and of a bearing to make women turn for a second look wherever he appeared. This companion seemed oblivious to the lashing of the sea, which turned the deck into a never-ending enemy of balance.

"How can you stand there without a care?" Charles demanded above the crash of the sea. "I should perish if I but let go my grip."

The taller man smiled enigmatically. "Practice, my friend, practice. Why aren't you below decks in your cabin? Unless one is used to the pounding of the sea, it can be anything but pleasant."

Charles laughed shortly. "Ah, Marcus, perhaps it is because I have learned so much from you these past months and years. Should I go, I fear you will perform some feat to which I shall not be privy."

The other man smiled at his young friend. "Should

such an occasion arise, I will be certain you learn of it, Charles. For a man of your gentle upbringing, you do seem an apt pupil for the acts of commoners."

"Commoners, indeed," Charles exclaimed, clutching wildly at the rail as the sea struck the ship a forceful blow. "You are no commoner, Marcus."

"No," Marcus agreed. "I am an American. The choice was mine and I have no regrets on that score."

"I should wonder not. How many of those who came as you did have done as well in as few years?"

"You flatter me. Let us go below and taste the grape before your head becomes so fogged with seawater you have me owning the country."

"You are too modest, Marcus. That, perhaps, is what women find so attractive about you. I can hardly wait to watch the lasses of London fall upon themselves at the sight of you."

Marcus fixed him with a humorous eye. "Is it possible that you've managed to take some wine early without my knowledge?"

Charles laughed heartily at the suggestion. Then, taking his friend's arm, he led the way below decks. When they were seated in his cabin, the youngest male Rothschild placed cups of wine on the table and said, "Unless my father has forgone the wine cellar of the halls, we'll soon be supping on much better than this."

"And what will the earl think of your bringing such as me into his home, Charles? Have you given that a thought?"

An expression of confusion swept over the younger man's face. "Why, how could he think anything but that I'd honored the house of Rothschild?"

"By bringing a commoner from across the sea to visit? I much doubt that he will make me as welcome as you seem to believe."

"You are my friend. When he learns the truth of what you are . . ."

"He shall not learn it from either of us, Charles," Marcus said. "Your word on that."

"Of course, Marcus. My word was given and it shall hold. I fail to see why, though."

"Reasons of my own, Charles. Let it go at that. And, should my presence become too uncomfortable for your family, I shall take myself elsewhere until you are ready to return."

"You'll wait for me, Marcus? I thought this to be nothing more than a whim of yours. I had no idea you were planning to wait for me to return."

"You do plan a return, do you not?"

"Of course. As soon as I discover the problem which has beset my father. Why, I would live noplace else of permanence. Much as I love this England, the new child country is vastly more exciting and promising than anything the mother could offer."

"And more dangerous, as you should have well learned."

"But that is part of the promise of the land, Marcus. You realize that, of course."

Marcus shook his head. "Several years ago, perhaps. Now, however, I've outgrown such thoughts. The fortunes are there to be made, but not by one who seeks them for the excitement and danger inherent in them. You have begun to show promise, Charles. But you still remain a portion the boy."

Charles's eyes glinted humorously. "Ah, and you have none of the daring in you? But then you are five years my senior. Age has a way of taking its toll on a man."

A chuckle slipped from the lips of the older man. "There are those who are old at twenty-seven, Charles. I had not featured myself as such. But perhaps you are right."

"Oh, come now, Marcus. It was said in jest. Surely you are not so sensitive about your age to resent being twenty and seven."

"Not sensitive, Charles. It is not the years a man lives but the miles he travels that age him. I was recalling several of those miles."

Charles sobered. "I see," he said thoughtfully. "I could, perchance, identify the miles you had in mind."

His friend nodded. "A few of them we shared together, Charles. Will you tell your family of them?"

"Now that is a question deserving of thought. There is the possibility that my father would not allow me to return to our country should he discover what has gone before in certain instances."

"My thought, also," Marcus agreed, getting to his feet and tipping the wine cup up to drain it. "Well, we are to arrive in your England early tomorrow. It would harm neither of us to glean some rest before the docking. Should you need me, I'll be in my quarters." With a nod of farewell, he left the cabin and made his way aft.

CHAPTER THREE

Lord Rothschild looked up from his perusal of a volume to nod to the manservant who had rapped softly on the open door. "Is the coach ready?" he asked when the man entered.

"Yes, my lord. Will Miss Penelope travel with you?"

"Of course," Rothschild said. "It is her brother we go to meet. Would that she be on time for once."

"Of whom are you speaking, Father?" Penelope asked from the doorway. "It is not I who constantly keeps you waiting. Come, or we shall be late. Charles would not forgive us for such a slight."

"Charles, I wager, will be so joyful at once again setting foot on English soil that he would not realize we were missing for some time. But you're right. We mustn't be late. Come." Taking her arm, he led her from the house to the waiting carriage.

"What will you tell Charles, Father?" she asked when the carriage was in motion.

"Of our condition? The truth, of course. His response can be no worse than that of his brothers. And he must know."

A thought before unknown to her crossed Penelope's mind. "Perhaps Charles has indeed amassed a fortune in America. Perhaps he will be of such wealth necessary to ransom Rothschild lands."

"Ah, child, you do dream. Charles was ever the addlepated one, you'll recall. I doubt the two years he's been across the sea will have changed him. No, had he, as you hoped, amassed a fortune, we would know of it."

"Charles was not addlepated," she argued in defense of her brother. "He cared not for titles and pomp—nor do I—but he was not addlepated."

Lord Rothschild patted his daughter's knee softly. "The choice of words was not apt. Better I had said he grew up with no responsibility for the claims of life."

Searching for and finding no genuine argument with the statement, Penelope sat silently. Finally, after several minutes, she asked, "Will they arrive on time, Father?"

"That, we shall soon discover," he answered. "We come now to the docks. Someone will know the whereabouts of the ship, I'm certain."

The words were lost on the girl. Her head was out the side window of the coach and she was pointing. "There he is, Father," she called into the wind. "He's just now mounting the dock. Oh, do tell the driver to hurry."

Chuckling at his daughter's delight, he answered, "Why, it would hardly do to run over poor Charles the first moment of his homecoming."

She had the door of the carriage open before the final turn of the wheels; then she was out and running toward the far end of the docks. Her bonnet slipped back to free the flow of her auburn hair. Her skirt, held several inches above her ankles, flapped in the breeze of her movement. "Charles," she called. "Charles, here!"

Caught up in the excitement of seeing her brother

for the first time in two years, she was oblivious to the dangers of everyday life on the docks. To the right of her, a barge loaded with casks of salt had begun the process of unloading. As she neared the vessel, barge workers, unaware of her, placed one of the huge casks on the roll board and freed it to make its way to the dock. The heavy cask immediately rolled down the slope of the board directly in Penelope's path. Suddenly one of the workers noted her danger and yelled, knowing as he did that it was too late. She stood little chance of being missed by the rolling projectile.

Behind the running girl, Lord Rothschild watched in horror as the cask and his daughter traveled toward their ungracious meeting. He, too, put voice to warning and began running as quickly as he could.

"Oh, great ghosts!" Charles exclaimed, paralyzed by the sight of his sister's plight. "Marcus, my sister—" But Marcus was no longer at his side.

Penelope became aware of the salt cask at the very moment her flying feet carried her into its path. Fear brought her to an instant stop, her hand going to her open mouth as the projectile moved to grind her under its weight. Suddenly she was struck at the waist by a weight which drove her backward to land solidly on the rough boards of the dock, her legs flying, her breath knocked from her.

The instant she struck the dock she was aware of a soft groan of pain and in the next instant realized that she was covered by a weight which could only be that of another person. Her hands came up to fend off her attacker as the salt cask rolled onward to the waiting stop posts at the side of the dock.

"Release me, sir," she gasped, pushing with all her might against the broad shoulders of her savior.

"Penelope, are you safe?" her father's voice intruded on her thoughts as the weight of the other's body left hers. Then her father's hands went under her shoulders and lifted her to her feet. "My daughter, are you all right?"

"I am, Father," she answered, her hands moving unconsciously to brush the dirt from her skirt.

"Penny, you vixen," Charles said, coming near her at a run. "You are as always, aren't you?" His glance left her before she could say a word of greeting. Then he was on his knee beside the tall, broad-shouldered stranger who had been the saving of his sister. "Marcus, what is it, old chap?" he demanded of the man, his voice carrying the heavy tone of concern normally reserved for close friends.

A smile crossed the face of the injured one and turned into a grimace of pain. "It would seem I've misjudged my speed and the speed of my foe."

"My good man," Lord Rothschild announced, kneeling beside him, "had it not been for you, my daughter would surely have been crushed under the weight of that infernal barrel. Lie as you are. I'll call help to lift you."

"I hardly believe that is necessary, sir," Marcus said. "If you will but ask your son to wipe the look of concern from his face and offer me his hand, I deem I will make it."

Penelope, still somewhat shaken by her experience, fixed the man with an appraising eye as her brother stood to offer him a helping hand. She was instantly aware that this man was unlike any of the dandies who frequented the halls as friends of her brothers. The thought flew through her shaken senses that, indeed, this one made her own brothers seem the worse for manly appearances. Then her eyes met his as he was pulled to his feet and the smile beneath those eyes of flashing blue brought color to her cheeks. Dropping her glance from his, she stepped forward to extend a hand. "My lord, my sincerest gratitude. Had it not been for you . . ."

"You would be as salted as a fish," the stranger laughed, reaching to take the proffered hand. "The legs which carry you in such haste are to be admired, my lady. Your awareness, however, is to be questioned." His head bent and his lips caressed her fingers as he spoke.

She colored at the statement and was about to retort when her brother Charles burst into laughter.

"Ah, Marcus, trust you to observe that which few others would have the presence to note at such a time. How is the leg, my friend?"

The lips left Penelope's fingers and the eyes again met hers. The laughter contained there made her draw her hand back suddenly. "My savior is a friend of yours, Charles?" she asked.

"Of the finest," Charles answered. "Father, Penelope, may I present Marcus Manners. Late of America, as I am myself. Marcus, my father, the Earl of Donley, and my overeager sister, Penelope."

With a wince of pain pulling at his lips, Marcus Manners turned and extended a hand to the earl. "The pleasure of this meeting is mine," he said with a slight bow.

"Hardly that, my young man," the earl exclaimed. "Hardly that. Why, it is my daughter's life you saved. What means of repayment can I make to you for your actions?"

"Perhaps a place to sit so the weight will be off this ankle," Marcus suggested with a smile. "I do believe I shall fall soon."

Instantly Charles was next to him, his hands raised to grip the wide shoulders in support. "Quickly, Father," he said, "help me to the carriage with him."

At that moment, one of the barge workers who had witnessed the daring rescue of the girl stepped ashore and, without a word, lifted Marcus in his arms. "Where to with this brave piece of baggage, guvnor?" he asked of Lord Rothschild.

"Here now, my good man," Marcus protested, "I'll not be treated as a child. I can make my own way."

"Sure and probably would that," the barge worker laughed. "But it is doubtful that it would do aught for the swelling of the ankle." Despite the protests of the man he carried and the ill-concealed smiles of Penelope and her brother, he moved Marcus to the carriage and placed him inside.

"Thank you, my good man," Rothschild said, offering a coin.

"That will not be necessary, my lord. It is little enough I've done for one such as that." With that, he turned back to his barge, leaving the group to themselves.

"Well, shall we go to the halls?" Rothschild asked of his children. "There is much to discuss and Lord Manners's ankle to see to."

"Mister Manners, if you please, my lord," Marcus requested as the four of them seated themselves in the carriage. "I have no use and little respect for the titles of your country."

"Of course," Rothschild answered, unabashed. His glance went to his daughter. "Yours is not the only such opinion within the bounds of this carriage."

Charles laughed. "Still outraging the kingdom with your antics, Pen?"

The girl blushed heavily, as all eyes were on her. With a slight kick at her brother, she said, "Beware, brother, the time still may be when I can make you cry Uncle."

At the threat, Marcus burst into laughter. "Charles, you made no mention of the fact that your sister—but a little bit of a lass—was your better in a match. It's little wonder you chose to sail across the seas to a land where the women were of easier mastering."

The four of them were laughing still when the carriage drew to a stop at the steps of Rothschild Halls. With the assistance of Charles and Lord Rothschild, and with Penelope watching every move made by them, the injured man was taken inside.

"We must have your ankle seen to immediately," Rothschild said when they'd seated the man in the library. "I shall—"

"Please, my lord," Marcus said in protest, " 'tis only a sprain. Nothing that a few days' rest will not see to. Do not bother so about it."

"The bones may be—"

"I'm certain they are not, my lord," Marcus said, "for broken bones are no stranger to the likes of me. There's little doubt that I should recognize such a thing if it were so."

Still uncertain, Rothschild nodded. "Very well, then, you shall remain in the halls and abed until the ankle gains strength." He turned to his daughter. "Penelope, see to it that the blue room is prepared for our guest and that Becky is at his side until he is again on his feet."

The girl seemed hesitant, and her nod of acquiescence was long in coming. "Yes, Father," she said.

"Well, and what bothers you about the blue room, my child? There is no other that will surpass it in the halls."

"Not the room, Father," she began, only to quiet herself at her brother's outburst of laughter.

"By all that's holy, Marcus, you've made a conquest of my sister. Now if she were but more to your tastes, the family Rothschild might well find itself invaded by the blood of—"

"Your sister is of rank befitting nobility, not the attentions of commoners," Marcus interrupted. He turned to the senior Rothschild. "There is no call for such ado, sir. I shall be perfectly well within a matter of days, I assure you. It is not my intent to burden you."

Rothschild studied him for a moment before turning his attention to his daughter. "Penelope, be off with you. See that Becky prepares for him. Move, dear girl," he prodded.

Her eyes snapping in anger at her brother, she turned and left them. Behind her, Charles chuckled in good humor.

"My apologies for my family, sir," Lord Rothschild said to Marcus. "It would seem that Charles's arrival has brought about a return of the madness which ruled both of them before his departure. It was my hope the experiences of this America would mature him."

Marcus smiled at him. "Your son has grown in many ways, my lord. His humor is affected, I suspect, by his pleasure at seeing his family."

At that moment, Becky entered the library to say, "The blue room awaits, my lord." Her eyes fell on Marcus and widened slightly in appreciation. She moved forward and dropped to curtsy before him. "My lord, savior of my mistress, yours is but to ask and I shall heed your wants."

Marcus sent a glance of embarrassment at Charles. Charles in turn again burst into laughter, saying, "Father, have you known the like? Less than a decent breath within our doors and the man has the ladies in a dither. I think it's a less than dull fortnight of healing we'll have in these halls."

Lord Rothschild shook his head in despair at his son's statements. "My apologies again, Mr. Manners. It would seem the Rothschilds are taking leave of their senses one by one. I can only hope that Charles's brothers have not been so infected." The statement seemed to call to mind an item of importance. Turning to Charles, he said, "Assist our friend to the blue room, Charles, and return here. Your brothers will be here shortly and there is much to discuss." He returned his glance to Marcus, dropped it to the girl, who was still curtsying, and said, "By all that's holy, woman, get your feet under you. You will be of little assistance to Mr. Manners like that."

The girl scrambled up and, her face tinged with red, made for the door of the library.

"I fear you shall have to be aware of that one, Mr. Manners," Rothschild said. "It would seem my son was correct in that, at least. The girl is overcome by you, and you have my sympathies. If she becomes bothersome, you have but to announce it to me." He reached to offer his hand as Marcus, with the help of Charles, got his feet under him and stood. "Again, though it is little enough in payment, my thanks for the life of my daughter."

Accepting the hand, Marcus nodded. "It would seem the family Rothschild is worthy of any and all actions of mine that would benefit them, my lord. The pleasure was mine. My gratitude for your concern."

"It is well that the family is in good health," Charles said as he assisted Marcus up the stairs. "I'd thought Father was failing when his message reached me."

"You are well nigh to being blind, Charles," Marcus answered. "Your father is consumed with worry over some matter. It would serve you well to return to him quickly. He has much on his mind to share with you."

Charles sobered at the words. Then he nodded shortly. "You are correct as usual, Marcus. Would that I could read another's feelings as you seem to do. I shall return and inform you of the news when Father and I are finished."

"I doubt the ills of the Rothschild family are to become common knowledge if your father can prevent it, Charles."

An expression of hurt crossed the younger man's features. "Marcus, I hardly believe my informing you could be termed common knowledge. No, my friend, you are to me as family."

"As you will," Marcus said, wincing slightly. "It would appear my blasted ankle will require a poultice. I must ask Mistress Becky if such is available."

The chuckle again came to Charles's lips. "Lord and you will make her day if you will but allow her to apply it. You'd best take care, Marcus, else you find yourself overtended from that quarter. She is a likely looking wench, to say the least."

"Your mind does settle in the lowest of the gutters at times. Your father does well to concern himself of your sanity. How much farther to this blue room where I am to be a prisoner?"

"We are here," Charles said with a flourish of his hand. "You have but to enter to partake of Becky's more personal ministrations."

When Marcus was abed, Charles smiled down at him, saying, "Your modesty surprises me, my friend. One would not believe you to be the rake of America. May I now recall Becky? I have no doubt she's been peeking around the edge of the door as you prepared for bed."

"Oh, begone with you, you fool," Marcus said in good humor. "Tell the lass I require a poultice for this accursed ankle."

"Right away, my lord," came the soft answer from the slightly open door.

The situation brought broad smiles to both men's faces. "Let it not pass without observance that I was at least partially correct, dear Marcus."

"Your father is waiting, Charles. From his manner, I suspect he needs you as he never has before. Go. I shall survive."

"You are correct, old friend," Charles agreed, turning from the bed. "I shall return and recount what occurs. Take care until then."

For several moments after the young man had gone,

Marcus lay silently surveying the room which was to be his kingdom for the next several days. He was engrossed in his surroundings when a slight sound at the doorway caught his attention.

"Beg pardon, my lord Marcus," Becky said. "The poultice is ready as you requested."

With a sigh of exasperation, Marcus said, "Well, bring it in, girl. And please, cease fluttering so."

An expression of satisfaction was on the maid's face as she presented the poultice and offered to apply it to the injured ankle. The expression became one of pleasure when he nodded his permission for her to tend him.

CHAPTER FOUR

Below the room of the injured man, Lord Rothschild sat with Penelope at his feet. Across from him, reclining in a chair, sat Charles. Rothschild had only just completed relating the facts of the situation to his son, and he now watched the young man's expression closely for a hint of what was to come.

"Well," Charles said after several long moments of silence. "It would seem we are indeed in somewhat of a tight corner, as Marcus would say. I assume, Father, that you have some plan of recovery in mind for the Rothschilds."

Lord Rothschild sat staring at this son of his in disbelief for a moment before saying, "I was wrong, Charles. You have matured in the new country. Whatever it is that has brought you to this point, I welcome it."

Charles shrugged. "Much of it is Marcus's doing, I fear. He will brook no pettiness from those who accompany him. But tell me, Father, what are our plans?"

Penelope raised her head from her father's knee to say, "See, Father, he's wonderful. Not at all like our brothers, who deem themselves of importance beyond all else."

"Hush, girl," Rothschild said, his attention on his youngest son. "As to my plans, my son, I know of naught to do other than call upon the baron and ask that he allow me to ransom the Rothschild name and inheritances over a period of time."

Charles stood silently for the length of two breaths. Then, with just a touch of fire in his manner, he said, "No, Father. Consulting with the baron is right and proper, but a Rothschild has never begged. If you do, indeed, intend to do so, then it behooves me to tell you that I have no intention of allowing you to leave the halls. I won't see you bow to this man."

"He cheated Father," Penelope stated.

"Silence," her father cautioned.

"Perhaps, Pen," Charles said. "However, whether it were by cheating or no, the fact remains that the man does control our fortunes. Father, tell me, are your eyes so bad that you could fail to detect that which my sister suggests?"

"I have no question as to the honesty of the baron," Rothschild answered. "Your sister is influenced by her emotions."

"I thought as much. For I remember well your talents at the gaming tables. Was it the bones or the cards, Father?"

"A bit of both, I fear," was the answer.

"Ah, well, no matter. When will you speak with this baron?"

In wonder at the mature method in which his son had accepted the facts of the situation, Rothschild straightened. "A messenger is even now on his way to ask when I might meet with the man. He should return momentarily."

"Then until his return, I would, if it pleases you, take my leave. I would like to discuss this with Marcus and glean his opinions."

His father's eyes opened wide at the statement. At his feet, Penelope's head came up swiftly. She stared at her brother as if he had taken leave of his senses.

"You would discuss the situation of the Rothschilds with an outsider? A commoner?" demanded the earl. "Are you mad?"

Charles colored slightly. "Father, Penelope, think what you will, but Marcus Manners is, in my opinion, the one person I should discuss it with. Unless dear old England has changed, word of the Rothschild plight was echoing from the corners within hours of the happening. Am I wrong, Father?"

There was a moment's embarrassed silence before the earl muttered, "You are not wrong, my boy. The news was off before I returned to the halls. That has nothing to do with the question of your sharing confidences with this . . . this . . ."

"Commoner," Charles supplied. "You have said that, Father. But within the last two years, I have owed my life to that man upstairs on at least two occasions. I won't bore you with the stories. But I will remind you that it was he, not a Rothschild, who was quick-witted enough this day to save our beloved Penelope from danger. It may well be that I burden him unfairly with our problems. He will, however, not look at it in that light."

"Your life was endangered?" Penelope breathed.

"As I said," he answered, "I doubt that our problem could be in better hands."

The earl reluctantly nodded. "It is not of his concern, but it seems you've grown in many ways. It would do me no good to say more against this, since I'm sure you'd do as you wish upon seeing your friend."

"Then I have your permission to discuss this with Marcus, Father?"

"Nay, you do not have. I only said I was aware of

the folly of trying to stop you." The old man's eyes dropped to Penelope. "What say you, Penelope?"

She was thoughtful for a heartbeat before saying, "Mister Manners seems quite able to handle himself in any situation, Father. Might it not be wise to make use of an outsider's view of our problem? Especially an outsider who, though a commoner, can look at our situation in honest appraisal without the emotions of family ties to deter him."

"Ah, well, it is like days of old. It seems the two of you are again outnumbering me on decisions. Very well, Charles, unfold the story of my idiocy to your friend. He can be no more critical than the rest of London."

"And, I'll wager, more sympathetic than two of your sons," Penelope muttered angrily.

"They were within bounds. It was their fortune I squandered."

"Then it was Charles's also," she argued. "And he did not attack you as did Monty and Rob. They are such total asses."

"Penelope," her father exclaimed. "Enough. Are you a common street woman to be using such language?"

"Would that I were," she exclaimed angrily. "Street women at least are allowed to think for themselves." With that, she got to her feet and hurried from the room.

"It would seem my dear sister is beside herself," Charles said. "Well, that in itself is not uncommon. By your leave, sir, if I may, I'll visit Marcus now."

The earl nodded. "Your brothers will arrive shortly. And the messenger from the baron, also. Then we shall determine the method of presenting our case."

With a nod of agreement, Charles left his father and made his way up the stairs to the blue room. Midway up the stairs, he met a red-faced, crying Becky on her way down. "Why, whatever has struck you, girl?" he asked.

"Oh, my lord," she choked, then sobbed heavily and swept past him down the stairs.

"By my soul," he exclaimed, scratching his head in wonder. "Will the mysteries of the female never end?" Turning back, he proceeded to his destination and entered Marcus's room. The greeting on his lips died when he became aware of his sister leaning over the bed.

"Well," he laughed, "and no wonder Becky was in such a state. You've used your station to usurp her pleasure in life, my sister."

She straightened and spun to face him. In one hand was a bowl of soup, in the other a deep spoon. Color flamed into her face as she said, "For your information, dear brother, she was making a complete botch of feeding our patient. Her attentions were more in presenting him a view of her ample bosom than of anything else."

Charles, aware of the pained expression on his friend's face, burst into raucous laughter. "Ah, Marcus," he said when he again had control, "what is this strange power you have over the lighter sex? I wager within hours you'll have the two of them at each other's throats."

"Enough," Marcus said. "The feeding as if I were a babe was a simple means of making the wench shut up and stop dithering around."

"Ah hah!" Charles exploded. "Now my sister is talking and dithering. It does not surprise me."

"Charles," Penelope exclaimed, "I—"

"I spoke of Becky," Marcus snapped. "Will you stop picking at your sister and allow her to relax?"

Still chuckling, Charles approached the bed and, with a twinkle in his eye, said, "Well, continue your feeding, sister. I think you'd be well advised to lower the neckline of your dress, however. Becky exposes more to the eye that is fetching than do you."

"Oh . . . oh . . ." she groaned. Then, with an anger-driven movement, she threw the bowl of soup directly at her brother.

"Well done, Lady Penelope," Marcus cheered as the broth ran down from Charles's face to his waist, soaking his attire.

For a long moment, the youngest of the Rothschild men stood looking down at the liquid which soiled him. Then, lifting his eyes to hers, he asked, "Am I to understand I've angered you, my lady?"

"Oh, you're incorrigible," she gasped. Then suddenly she burst into laughter. "You're a sight, Charles. Do go change before Father sees you."

"That is indeed a noteworthy suggestion. I shall return shortly. Meanwhile, sister, do something about the unattractive bosom of that dress." He turned quickly to leave. The spoon bounced off the door frame as he hurried through it. His laughter drifted back to the blue room as he made his way to change.

Blushing heavily, Penelope turned to a stern-faced Marcus. "My apologies, sir. My brother is, I fear, a rapscallion."

"One who wishes, for once, to best his sister, if I'm a judge," Marcus said. "Truly, it was a sight to behold when you souped him."

"I'm sorry," she said, her color receding. "I'll get you more soup."

"Please, my lady, no more. As I said, it was but a method of calming the lass. Hunger is not a problem to me at present."

She nodded. "It would seem my brother is more than a bit right. We females do seem to be crowding you. My apologies, sir."

His eyes widened at the frank admission. Then his lips spread into a smile. "My lady, would that every woman I'd met could be as honest as you."

She relaxed visibly at his words. Her smile matched his and she asked, "Would you be willing to humor a brazen lass and tell her some of what the ladies of the new world are about?"

"You refer to their dress, I suppose."

She nodded. "True. That, and their station. Are they so bound up in the noble ivy of the past that they can do nothing but sew and sit at the spinet?"

Her words brought a chuckle from him. With a shake of his head, he said, "There are those who are, as you say, bound by old fashions. Many, however, are honest helpmates to their husbands. Others are, as in London, occupied with sins of the flesh. No offense, my lady."

She sobered. "And none taken, sir. Tell me, are they as corseted as the barrel-big ladies of the court?"

"Some are," he admitted laughingly. "Others are as yourself, slim to the point where whalebone is not a necessity."

She blushed again and asked shyly, "And sir, which of all those you have mentioned did Charles find attractive?"

"And what she really wishes to know is which of them attracted you, Marcus," Charles said from the doorway. "Lord pray she doesn't turn with another bowl of soup in her hands."

Without facing him, she retorted, "Oh, Charles, stop acting the fool. You intended to relate something of importance to Marcus, I recall."

"That I did," he answered. "Be gone with you, sister. We have things to discuss."

"I'll not leave. It's a Rothschild I am and entitled to know what is about for my family."

Marcus met his friend's eyes and smiled. "It would seem your sister deserves more to serve her life in the new America than in a confining England, Charles. Admit her her due. She is of the family and thereby more deserving than I of information concerning it."

"She is a lass," Charles protested.

"Amazing!" Marcus said. "It's absolutely uncanny the effect the touch of one's feet on English soil has upon one."

"What are you talking about, Marcus?" Charles demanded.

"I speak of the sudden amount of narrowness your mind has taken on since you first stepped ashore this day. It would seem that the years I've worked with you have gone for naught."

Charles reddened under the criticism. His glance went to Penelope, who stood, still angry, beside the injured man's bed. "My apologies, sister. Marcus, as usual, is correct. It seems I have reverted to the ways of the Englishmen of old." He returned his attention to Marcus. "You may live to rue this day you force me to shower liberality on this particular lass, Marcus. Well, shall we go to it?"

"If you think it wise, Charles. I doubt that your father agreed to your disclosure, though."

"Tell our problems to a commoner?" Penelope aped the earl.

"I thought as much. Then why, pray tell, are you about to do so?"

"It's simple, sir," the girl answered before her brother could speak. "You are not of Rothschild blood. Even though you are a commoner, you have impressed my brother with your imagination. Yours will be the views of a disinterested party and more than likely much closer to the truth than ours of prejudice."

He nodded in understanding. "Very well, then, let's get to it. Charles, Lady Penelope, draw up some chairs."

Some time later, when between the two of them they had explained the problems of the Rothschilds to him, Marcus sat thinking. Finally, after long minutes of such silent thought, Penelope could be patient no longer. Pushing herself from the chair, she said, "Are we in such peril that there is no answer forth-coming from your friend, Charles?"

Marcus met her glance and smiled. "Sit, lass. Else I shall have to instruct you in the ways of commoners thrashing children. I think you would find it anything but pleasant to your posterior."

"Hah!" she snorted. "Would you like the other ankle to match your injured one, sir?"

"Hush, Pen," Charles ordered. Then to Marcus, "Well, friend, what of it? Is there something the Rothschilds can do to improve their lot?"

"The baron, being Prussian, is not likely to be sympathetic to your father's cause," Marcus answered. "I think the earl would do well to look to what he has of value that the baron wants."

"Of value?" Penelope gasped. "In truth, sir, did you not hear my brother and me explain that all the Rothschild wealth is at the moment in the baron's control?"

"I heard. I fail to believe it, though. Let us wait until your father returns from his visit with the baron and discover what it is that has been overlooked by all of you."

Irritation crept into the girl's eyes. She swung on her brother. "What more can he do? Take the clothes from our backs?"

Charles, his studious glance on his friend, shook his head. "Marcus, what is it you speak of that is of value to the Rothschilds? Our lands, our stables, our finances and investments, these all are under bond to the baron. There is nothing else, save, as Pen pointed out, the clothes on our backs."

Marcus held up a palm for silence. "A question, Charles. If the earl and the baron are long-standing foes, why was the earl at the games with him?"

"But they are not," Charles protested. "The baron has been in England only a year, from what my father tells me." His glance shifted to Penelope, who nodded.

"And of the others he has dealt ruin to, are they many?"

"I know of no others that have fallen to him to such an extent, sir," the girl answered. "Surely, had there been such a case, news of it would have traveled as it did of father."

Marcus nodded wisely. "Then it would seem there must be a reason for your father to have been singled out as the object of the baron's enmity. Tell me, my lady, has the baron visited Rothschild Halls since his coming to England?"

She thought but a minute before saying, "Only once, sir. It was on the occasion of my last birthday. Father gave a party in my honor, and the baron was invited as a guest of one of father's friends."

"Then I suspect the baron most surely decided on that occasion that he should have something the Rothschilds have. He has, I wager, planned well for the campaign, and included in his plans was the cheating of your father at the gaming tables."

"Oh, Marcus," Charles protested. "The earl has been a champion gamester at both cards and the bones for as long as I can remember. I find it difficult indeed to—"

"And therefore the more confident that he could never be cheated," Marcus interrupted. "That and the knowledge of the small things which indicate to any true gamester that luck is beginning to turn in his favor. Should a man turn these indicators to his own use by proper manipulation of the cards, it could well lead someone to destruction if he didn't expect it." He paused a moment in thought, then added, "Tell me, Charles, was it the bones or the cards which cost your father most dearly of the Rothschild fortunes?"

Charles's glance went to his sister, who shook her head in ignorance of the answer. Again meeting the eyes of Marcus, he said, "In truth, Marcus, I don't know. Would you like me to ask my father?"

"It would help to know. But I doubt that he would freely give the information if he were to know you intended it for me."

"There you are in error, sir," Lord Rothschild announced from the door of the bedroom. "For several minutes now, I've listened as a thief listens, and for that I offer my apologies. However, I think perhaps that my two youngest were correct in their desire to inform you of our plight. And though I, too, wonder at the valuable you suspect the baron is desirous of, I will give you the answer to your query. The baron and I spent several hours gaming with the bones. It was only after such a time that he suggested we turn our hands to the cards, and it was then that I foolishly allowed the Rothschild fortunes to slip."

Marcus nodded. "I thought as much. 'Tis much easier to befuddle one with them than with the bones."

Lord Rothschild sighed. "In truth, I—" He broke off as a manservant appeared at the door and informed him that the messenger from the baron had arrived. With a grimace and a nod at those present in the room, he said, "We will shortly be informed as to when I may have conference with the baron. Charles, if you will accompany me."

"Certainly, Father," Charles answered, his glance going to Penelope in question.

The girl was thoughtful for a moment before saying, "Attend the messenger. I shall stay and see to our guest's wants. We shall both await the news from the baron."

A knowing smile on his face, Charles bowed shortly and turned to accompany his father.

When the two had left the bedroom, Penelope turned her attentions to Marcus. "Well now, and you were telling me of the women in the colonies when my brother made his unruly entrance. Would you continue, sir?"

"My lady, there is little else to tell. Many work in the fields with their mates. Others cook and sew and do household chores to assist the servants—if, indeed, there are servants in the house. There are those, as I stated, who prefer the old methods to the new and remain the genteel ladies of leisure."

"And do their men look upon these women with the same respect an Englishman bestows upon his chosen one?"

"More so," he answered. "And you err, my lady. For most of the gentlemen of which you speak are English."

She nodded. "More so? How is that, sir? How could any show more respect than is shown in mother England?"

His dry chuckle was as rock on wood. " 'Tis the respect of joint venturers, my lady. In many—aye, most—cases, the husband and wife are partners, both of whom are working toward a common goal. I think you would find it confusing."

There was a faraway look in her eyes. "Confusing, perhaps, but refreshing even more for the confusion. Oh, that I might be accepted as a useful portion of whatever my husband partakes, should I ever betake such a thing."

"You have plans of betrothal, my lady?"

She blushed. "The dandies of my acquaintance are of a turn to desire the more abundantly endowed than I, sir. Which is as well, since I respect none of them."

"Harsh words for the gentlemen of the courts, my lady."

"But true, as you would see if you could study them. 'Twould be interesting to note your thoughts concerning them."

His lips turned up in a smile. "They are not unknown to me, my lady. And in many such instances, your term *dandy* is complimentary to their usefulness. They offer little to the world other than the high-handed touch of the aristocrat who expects all for naught."

She met his smile and seated herself on the bed. "And with that honest appraisal, sir, you become entitled to call me by my given name. I tire of the title 'my lady.'"

"And I of the title 'sir,'" he answered. "A trade: You shall call me Marcus and I shall refer to you as . . . what shall it be—Penelope, Penny, Pen? I've heard all three since entering Rothschild Halls."

"I prefer Penny, Marcus," she answered with lowered eyes. "Though whichever is easiest for you will serve."

"Then Penny it shall be," he answered, his attention going to the door of the room. "And what could Becky want of us?"

The maid stood in embarrassed silence for a moment after his query. Then, her eyes on the floor, she announced, "Your elder brothers have arrived, my lady. The earl would have you in attendance with them."

A frown of irritation swept over Penelope's features. Then, with a smile at Marcus she slid from the bed, saying, "It would seem the family cannot do without me, Marcus. I shall return the soonest I can. Rest comfortably." She turned away and met the expression of pleased expectancy in the eyes of Becky. "Well, get on about your duties, girl," she said as she passed to the hallway.

"Yes, my lady," the maid answered, her eyes on Marcus.

A slight groan of defeat left the lips of the injured man as he noted the look in the eyes of the bosomy maid. "I would rest now if I may, Becky," he said in hopes of belaying her intentions.

"Ah, sir, and I would be amiss were I to allow your injury to pass without inspection. 'Twill take but a moment to be certain that the poultice is properly adjusted." She was at the bedside rolling the covers back as she finished speaking.

CHAPTER FIVE

It was some time later when Marcus, feigning sleep to ward off the overindulgent maid, heard Charles whisper, "He sleeps, my brothers. His introduction to the eldest of the family sons will have to wait."

"Rothschilds must await the convenience of a commoner?" a male voice somewhat coarser than Charles's demanded without semblance of quiet.

"Enter, Rothschilds," Marcus said, coming to a sitting position in the bed. "We commoners welcome you."

Instantly at his words, a man inches shorter than Marcus stepped over the threshold to cast a glance around the room. "The blue room?" this one asked. "It seems the commoners demand the finest when injured."

"Enough of your ways, Montgomery," the earl snapped from behind the man. "Had it not been for Mr. Manners, your sister would be naught but mush at this moment."

"And," Charles added, entering the room accompanied by the eldest of the Rothschild heirs, "commoner he may be, but a warning word, my brother.

His lack of respect for titles and those who hold them dear is exceeded only by his acumen with weapons and fists. Take heed, lest this commoner stand on his good ankle and thrash you."

Montgomery turned, an expression of distaste on his face. "I think your friend would find it not to his liking should such a thing occur, Charles. You were ever the impressionable one."

"Enough, I said," the earl demanded. "The man is a welcome guest in the halls. You will afford him the respect you would any equal—else, I fear, you will not be allowed to escape my wrath." He crossed to the bedside, saying, "It has been decided that I shall indeed call upon the baron and beseech him to allow repayment of my debts over a period of time."

"What is this, Father?" Robroy demanded. "Grant you, the man deserves our respect for the saving of Pen, but are we indebted to discuss the Rothschild shame with him as well?"

Marcus raised his eyes to meet those of the eldest Rothschild son. "The Rothschilds are not in my debt at all," he said. "But I am curious as to your meaning with the use of the word *shame*."

"It is none of your concern," Rob huffed. "And I will thank you to call me by title."

The beginning of a smile worked at the lips of the injured man. He was about to speak when Penelope swept into the room, breathless from her swift climbing of the stairs. He held his tongue until she'd come to a stop beside her father and looked down at him. Then, the smile taking on a new meaning, Marcus nodded his head at her and said, "Penny, you do make haste at all times."

"Penny! Penny!" Montgomery exclaimed. "Oh, by the saints, what liberties are we to allow this peasant for doing no more than any other would?"

The girl turned on him, her face flaming in anger.

"You, Montgomery, are a total ass. It is by my request that Marcus refers to me as Penny. Must you and Rob forever be such dolts?"

"Out, the two of you," the earl ordered. "Out and away from the man. Never have I imagined the Rothschilds could become such boors. Out, I say."

With a glance of disgust passing between them, the two eldest of the clan turned away toward the door. Robroy, on the threshold, turned back to say, "Our thanks for aiding our sister in her time of need, commoner." Then he was gone.

"Mr. Manners," the earl began, "I . . ."

"No words are necessary, my lord," Marcus said. "The actions of your sons speak not of your training but of the example set by society for them to follow. Now, if I may, what of this meeting with the baron?"

Rothschild hesitated only a second before saying, "It has been decided that I shall call upon the baron on the morrow. As my youngest son has said, Rothschilds do not beg. I will, however, attempt to reach an equitable understanding with the man that will benefit him and return the material fortunes of the Rothschilds to our control."

Marcus let his glance fall on Charles, who shrugged, saying, "There seems naught else to do, Marcus. Would that I could strike flint and put a ball in the man, but Father will have none of that."

"My son is overzealous, I fear," the earl said. "His life in America seems to have made a ruffian of him, if nothing else."

"Then am I also a ruffian, Father?" Penelope asked. "For were it possible, I too would have the man dead."

Rothschild exchanged a glance with Marcus. "What is a father to do with two such as these, Mr. Manners? The girl is, indeed, the ruffian I supposed Charles of becoming."

"If it is as we suspect, my lord, the man truly deserves whatever becomes him. It would do the family

Rothschild little good, though, if he were to receive death at the hands of one of its members." He hesitated momentarily, then asked, "If I might, my lord— were your oldest sons of the feeling that you should meet with this baron?"

"Oh, that they were," Penelope said quickly. "Those two would, if it were not for Charles and myself, have Father on his knees before the fat Prussian pig. They think only of themselves."

"Theirs is a concern for the family," the earl corrected. "You misread their motives, girl. Hold your tongue." His attention went again to Marcus. "You are in need of rest, sir. The day has been a tiring one for all of us. When my conference with the baron is concluded, we may then have reason to rejoice. Until then, there is nothing to be done by us."

"The party, Father," Penelope reminded.

"Ah, yes, the party. It is with the greatest of pleasure, sir, that I invite you to attend, as best your ankle will allow, a party in honor of the homecoming of my son. Your presence will indeed serve the Rothschilds well."

"My ways are not those of the nobility, my lord," Marcus answered.

"And thanks be for that," Penelope said. Turning to Charles, she added, "Brother mine, is this friend of yours of such station that he considers the Rothschilds and their galas to be beneath him?"

Charles came forward to face Marcus. "In truth, Marcus, I have remained silent because of a thought which has come to me. There is a blind cripple in the town. He uses a crutch made from a tree limb. You shall have such a thing by the morrow. As to the party and my sister's concern for your attendance, it is decided. You will attend on one foot or I shall allow Penelope to kick your good ankle."

Marcus laughed at the threat and at the flush of color which swept into the girl's face. "It would seem

I have no choice in the matter. Very well, my lords and my lady, I will attend your gala. Would that I do nothing to bring shame upon your family." He raised a fist to his mouth to cover a yawn. "I fear you were correct, my lord earl. The day has had its way with my strength."

"The cook has prepared roast highland lamb, Marcus," Penelope said hopefully. "Would you sup before sleep?"

"Ah, Pen," Charles said in humor, "allow the man a moment's respite from your eager attentions."

She was about to retort when Marcus said quietly, "I would be honored and, I am certain, well fed if you would join me in the meal, Penny."

Charles faced his friend and, with a shake of his head, warned, "You know not what you do, Marcus. The lass's head will fill with dreams and she will be as a second skin to you. You'll not be able to get shed of her."

"Enough, my son," the earl said. "Your humor has cost your sister enough for one day. Let us out of here. I, too, feel the pangs of hunger gnawing at me."

Penelope had remained silent since the invitation from Marcus. As her father and brother turned to leave, she curtsied, saying, "I shall return shortly with our meal, Marcus."

Charles turned back to them. "By all that's holy, Marcus, you've made my sister into a servant girl before my eyes. I feel I shall regret bringing you from America." His cautious glance was on his sister as he spoke.

She spun, her eyes searching for a missile to hurl at him. "I'll . . ."

Her brother's laughter answered her as he made his way out and down the stairs.

"My brother would ever pester me, Marcus," she explained. "Would that he were more the adult, as are some others."

"Would that every lass had a brother who loved her so," Marcus answered. "You mentioned highland lamb, I believe."

"Oh! My brother robs me of my thoughts. I shall return shortly, Marcus, and we shall sup together." Turning, she left the room, her thoughts forming what she considered a daring plan. No sooner had she left the room of the injured man than she called for Becky. When Becky appeared at the stairs, Penelope signaled urgently for the maid to join her, and together they made their way to Penelope's chambers.

"What is it, m'lady?" Becky asked as the door of the chamber closed behind them.

"Quickly, Becky, I must change. The blue silk, I believe. Hurry, girl." She was already slipping from the plain gown she'd thought sufficient for meeting her returning brother.

"The blue silk, m'lady? Is it a party you are attending?"

"No time for your questions, Becky. The blue silk. And then you must do something with this hair of mine."

A chuckle escaped the lips of the servant girl. "He is a fetching one for a certainty, ma'am. It was with hope I myself looked upon him. I fear he was not caught up with me, though."

"What are you babbling about, Becky?" Penelope demanded, color flooding over her.

"Why, the friend of Master Charles, m'lady. Who else?" Becky answered, laying the blue silk across the bed.

"I dress not to attract the glances of Mr. Manners," Penelope told her. " 'Twas this morning I donned the simple dress. The day's happenings have been the worse for it."

"Of course, m'lady. But wasn't it the blue silk you so disliked because of its bareness, m'lady?"

For an instant, anger flared in the eyes of Penelope.

Then, a conspiratorial smile on her lips, she said, "We ladies are the conniving ones, are we not, Becky?"

Becky nodded. "We are that, ma'am. And a good thing for the gentlemen that we are, else they would never know happiness."

A concerned expression crossed Penelope's face. "Is the blue silk too brash, Becky?"

"Oh, not at all, ma'am. Would that your bosom made a better job of it, but that is of no bother. The gown was made to fit you. And the gentlemen will forget his ankle upon gazing at you dressed so."

"We must hurry, Becky," Penelope urged. "Help me with the gown."

Some twenty minutes later, aware of an unaccustomed coolness at her shoulders and throat, Penelope reentered Marcus's bedroom followed by a manservant bearing a large platter of food and drink. She stood aside for the servant to lower the tray for the injured man's inspection.

"The small table, Penny," he said with a nod. "I believe it will serve us well for this delicious-looking meal."

She turned quickly from his glance, glad to have her back to him and her exposed bosom out of his sight. Removing the trivialities from the table he'd indicated, she moved it to a position beside the bed, doing her best to keep from bending forward.

Her color was bright when the manservant placed the tray on the table and took his leave. "Doesn't it look delectable, Marcus?" she asked, attempting to keep her discomfiture from her voice.

"It is indeed a meal of which anyone would be desirous," he agreed as she seated herself across from him. He lifted a bowl of food from the tray and began eating. His glance on her was filled with humor until she attempted to reach the bread without breaking the rigidity of her back. Finally she was forced to bend toward him. Her hand came up to push against the sparse bodice of the dress as she leaned forward. Her color rose suddenly and her eyes went to his face.

"'Tis delicious fare," he said, smiling, "but, alas, England is as I'd recalled."

She straightened, searching him for signs of humor at her unease. "And how is that, Marcus?" she asked.

"Damp and cool in the evening," he answered. "I wonder that you aren't chilled to the bone. Wouldn't you prefer a shawl to cover your shoulders?"

Her relief at his words was only too apparent. Getting up from her chair, she turned toward the door, saying, "You're correct, Marcus. I do feel a chill. I shall return shortly." She took two steps and turned, her eyes suddenly filled with anger, her color high. "You make jest of me, Marcus. 'Twas not the cold you were concerned with when Becky displayed her abundance to you."

An expression of pity crossed his features. "Ah, Penny lass, 'tis two different persons of which you speak. You are not a Becky, thank the Lord, nor is Becky a Penny—though she would have it that way were it within her power, I think. I make no sport of you, lass. Yours is not the beauty of the Beckys of this world, nor of the court wenches who deem it their duty to expose all possible of their bodies for the evaluation of male eyes. You are a lovely lass who need not partake of such frivolity to catch the eyes of any man who is in attendance. Now go, put something over your shoulders lest you catch your death of cold."

She hesitated only a moment longer before turning and running from the room.

Behind her, Marcus sat, still holding the bowl of food, an expression of thoughtfulness on his features. Aloud, he said, "Ah, Marcus, you'd best look to your heartstrings lest that one control them."

CHAPTER SIX

The brilliance of full daylight flowing into the chamber brought Marcus from sleep. He stretched widely and yawned, enjoying the comfort of the huge bed. The happenings of the previous day were brought to mind by a twinge of pain from his ankle. His thoughts went to the problems of the Rothschild family. "I think the earl will be much distressed when he returns from his conference with the baron," he told himself.

His thoughts were interrupted by the stealthy opening of the chamber door. "I am awake," he called. "Enter."

"And about time," Charles said, stepping into the room. "We'd thought you dead and were preparing a box for your remains."

"In such a bed as this, one finds deep sleep a simple thing to achieve. What is the hour?"

"You've slept the morning away, my friend. And in that time, others have been working in your stead." He turned back to the doorway and produced a crutch of smoothed wood. "Behold. Your leg of necessity. Isn't it a work of art?"

Accepting the crutch, Marcus ran a hand along its

length. "It is a work, I'll agree. As to the artful side of it, I hesitate to comment. What a crashing bore to be burdened with such a thing. Ah, well, I suppose I must. Help me to my feet, Charles."

Moving to help his friend, Charles glanced at the ankle and exclaimed, "By jove, Marcus, the poultice has apparently done its work well. The swelling of the ankle is all but gone. Has the pain lessened as well?"

Cautiously Marcus allowed his weight to settle on the ankle. His lips tightened in pain momentarily, then he smiled at Charles. "To stand without movement there is but a little pain. Your poultice maker works miracles, Charles. Now let me try the crutch and see if I shall be able to navigate."

With the crutch in position under his arm, he took one cautious step and then another. "I do believe I shall manage," he laughed. "I would have my clothing, Charles."

"Do you plan to leave this chamber, Marcus? Would it not be better to wait another day?"

"With the crutch, the ankle can be exercised, my worrisome friend. My clothing, please."

"Very well, Marcus. Your powers of recovery are astounding, as is most everything you do. I'll return with your baggage shortly. But, until I do, it's back to bed with you. I'll not come under the lash of my sister's tongue for allowing you to fall in my absence."

Marcus allowed himself to be assisted back to the bed before saying, "About this sister of yours, Charles. It strikes me that, though it is all in good humor, you do try her overmuch. She is of the age when such teasing might upset her."

Charles straightened to fix his friend with an evaluating eye. "I say, Marcus, can it be that you are becoming infatuated with Pen?" He smiled broadly. "Lord have it, it would be a marvelous thing if the two of you were to— The family Rothschild would—"

"Hang me by my thumbs, as it were," Marcus interrupted. "Stop your insane dithering. She is but a child."

"A child of eighteen, Marcus. Ah, you didn't know. I supposed I had made mention of her years. She is but four years my junior."

"I was not aware of it," Marcus admitted. "It has no bearing on the matter, though. Your sister concerns me only as she is a kind lass and, I hope, a friend."

"Of course, Marcus," Charles smiled. "Well, I shall get your baggage. Pray do not attempt to remove yourself from the bed. I fear your . . . ah . . . kind lass would have my head if you were to add to your injury." Chuckling, he turned and left the room.

"Dunce!" Marcus snorted, aware that he'd allowed his pleasure to show at the mention of the girl's age.

When his clothing had been brought, Marcus, with the assistance of Charles, donned leisure apparel and once again placed the crutch under his arm. "Now, let us see if I can traverse the stairs," he said, moving unsteadily toward the door. Over his shoulder, to the ever-watchful Charles, he asked, "And what of your father, Charles? Has he gone to his appointment with the baron, yet?"

"Long ago, Marcus. I fear Father will find the man a demanding bore."

"I, too," Marcus agreed. "Well, if I am to attend your gala, it would seem I must practice walking with three legs. I appear as unsteady as did you on the deck of the ship."

"Marcus," the younger man began hesitantly, "it is, I know, none of my concern and certainly only your own. But has the touch of English soil made no difference to you?"

"Any difference will be made my necessity, Charles."

Together, with the younger man leading, Charles and Marcus made their slow, uncertain way down the stairs. When they reached the lower floor, Marcus breathed deeply. "That will take some practice, Charles. However, I do believe I shall master it. Where to?"

"It does seem, my friend, that you have captured my sister's heart. Ah well, such was to be expected."

"What has that to do with anything?"

"She awaits you on the terrace. As a matter of fact, Marcus, I, too, await you. We would breakfast with you, under her orders." He chuckled. "She did, praise God, allow Father to dine before he left. When she saw the crutch early this day, she asked me of the possibility of your descending the stairs, and like a fool, I assured her you would. As a result, my innards do feel that I've neglected them. Shall we?" Still chuckling, he led the way through the house to an open terrace surrounded by flowers and overlooking the rolling lands of the senior Rothschild.

"Marcus," Penny exclaimed happily when her eyes fell on him. "Your ankle . . ."

"Doing quite well, Penny," he assured her. "Thanks to the ministrations and care of yourself and the others in the halls." He raised his eyes from hers to scan the surrounding countryside. "Beautiful," he murmured.

"This is my favorite of all the views on Rothschild estates," she said. "Will you breakfast with Charles and myself, Marcus?"

With a glance at a smug-looking Charles, he nodded. "It would seem I have an appetite, Penny. Charles, I believe I shall require assistance in seating myself this first time."

The meal was barely finished when the sound of carriage and steeds came to them. Penny, her head cocked to listen, asked, "Can that be Father returning so soon? If it is, it would seem he is accompanied by men on horseback." She got to her feet and smiled at Marcus. "I shall see who it is."

When she'd swept into the house, Charles laughed heartily, saying, "Ah, Marcus, you have her bound hand, foot, and heart. I find sympathy for my little sister in her ignorance of worldly ways."

"And I a sympathy for her for the actions of her brother," Marcus replied as the girl returned. Swinging his attention to her, he asked, "And what is it that has you appearing so crestfallen, Penny?"

"Father is returned. By his expression, he is about to be set upon by hordes of ogres. He would like you and Charles to attend him in the library."

"Bad news from the baron, I suspect," Marcus said, getting awkwardly to his feet. "Blast this leg and all that goes with it."

"Is the baron with Father?" Charles asked, getting to his feet. "There were the sounds of riders."

"Our brothers," the girl answered. "In none too fine a mood, from their looks. I daresay they are impatient to know what passed between Father and the baron."

"Well, then, we shall have to protect him from them, shall we not, Pen?" Charles said. "Come, let us brave our brothers in the library."

"You are certain your father asked that I attend?" Marcus asked.

"Oh, of a certainty, Marcus, amid the protests of my two older brothers, of course. But he was adamant. You shall attend. Come."

"I have an ill feeling about this," Charles said as they made their way into the house and to the library.

"Trouble may come soon enough," Marcus advised. "But let us wait and hear what the problem is."

The door of the library was open when they approached. From inside, the voice of the eldest son could be heard. "Am I not the heir of the Rothschilds, Father? Am I, as such, to have no say as to who is informed of our problems? A commoner, by God! It is unheard of in all England's history."

"Were it not for commoners, my son," the earl's voice answered, "there would be no lands or fortunes for the Rothschilds to call their own. It was commoners who made England what she is. The nobility only gives direction."

"Wise man," Marcus murmured as they entered the room.

"Well, I will not be a party to this!" Montgomery exclaimed agreement with his brother. "If you persist in allowing this . . . this . . . *peasant* to invade the interests of the Rothschilds, I shall leave."

"Well said," Robroy agreed, his glance sweeping over the three who had just entered the library. "Father?"

"I fear your sons are correct, my lord," Marcus said before the old man could speak. "Their concern is well founded. I shall take my leave."

"Hold," the earl ordered. "You shall remain, Mr. Manners. If my sons persist in their childish ways, they may indeed take their leave of the halls. But they will have no part in the decision of what is to be done. Nor will they share in the knowledge of what has passed between the baron and myself." His eyes were burning on his two eldest sons as he spoke.

"And," Charles added, "should either of you choose to use your sharpened tongue against my friend again, I personally will see to you."

"Younger brother seems to believe himself a man," Montgomery said sarcastically. "I may be forced to instruct him in the proper treatment of his elders."

"You are fine ones to speak of treatment of elders," Charles snapped. "This man standing here is your father. Show him the respect you would receive from others." He turned to his father. "Father, what is it that has rattled you so?"

"The baron is a lunatic in his demands," the earl answered, seating himself. "There is no sense in the man."

Penny, concern for her father apparent in her expression, crossed to kneel beside his chair. "What is it, Father? What does the man demand?"

The earl's eyes raised to fix themselves on Marcus's face. "Our friend was correct when he surmised that the baron wished something of great value from the Rothschilds."

"Oh, by all that's holy," Robroy exclaimed hopefully, "then there is a method of returning the Rothschild fortunes to their rightful place?"

"There is," the earl said sadly. "However, the method is one that denies consideration by any gentleman of this house."

"Nonsense!" Montgomery exclaimed. "Whatever it is the baron desires of us can surely be supplied. My lord, he has the lot, as it were. Whatever else there is is of no—"

"He wishes your sister in marriage," the earl interrupted.

Silence, thick and heavy, settled over the room at the statement. For the space of several heartbeats, no one spoke. Then, his eyes going to Marcus, the earl asked, "You knew, did you not, my friend?"

Marcus nodded shortly. "I suspected, my lord. I hoped it would be otherwise. It did, however, seem the one logical thing the man would plan so well toward."

Penny stood with mouth open, staring at her father. Suddenly she gasped, "Father, he said that?"

"Demanded," the earl corrected, "as if I were the lowest of peasants. *Demanded* that your troth be announced at the gala on the morrow. The man is mad. No Rothschild will be so handled."

"Preposterous!" Charles exclaimed. "Does the man think we can be handled as putty?"

The two eldest stood silently for a long moment. Finally Robroy, with a glance at Montgomery, said,

"Let us not be overly hasty in this consideration, Father."

The earl's head came up. "What? The eldest of my children would submit a member of his family to slavery as the price of his lands?"

"Hardly slavery," Montgomery put in. "She is, after all, of marriageable age. She will certainly wed at some time. The baron is nobility, and as such is worthy of her."

"He is a pig," Penelope screamed. "I will not hear you speak that way."

"Oh, begone, girl," Robroy ordered. "Your view is of no importance. This is a matter to be settled by the Rothschild men." He turned to his father. "Father, would that you remove this commoner from our ranks that we might freely discuss this matter."

"Marcus stays," Charles said flatly. "As does Penelope. Are you as mad as this baron?"

"Father," Penelope pleaded, "you cannot listen to them. The man is of an age that matches your own."

"I do not intend that my daughter should become the wife of such a scoundrel," the earl said.

"You do not intend?" Montgomery demanded. "You, who have in a moment's idiocy lost all that rightfully belonged to us? I think, Father, you'd best look to your senses. Not only have you, in a manner, purloined what belongs to Rob, Charles and myself; you have, in the same flick of a card, made waste of any dowry our sister could expect. Consider, sir, our position."

"It is beyond discussion or reason," the earl said, a bit sadly. "I—"

"If you will, Father, might we discuss this in private?" Robroy asked. "Your insistence on—"

"No need to continue in that vein," Marcus said. "I will, by your leave, my lord, retire to the grounds. This is indeed business to which I should not be privy."

The earl was thoughtful for a moment before saying, "My apologies, sir. It seems I have made use of your shoulders to share the burden of the family. My thanks for your assistance to this point."

With a nod, Marcus turned to go.

"And our sister, Father?" Robroy asked.

"Indeed, we are all concerned for her best, Father. She need not enter into the discussion of what is to be done," Montgomery agreed.

An expression of disgust on his face, the earl eyed his daughter. Finally he nodded. "Go, Penelope. Show our friend Marcus around the estate. But don't concern yourself about the doings in this room, for I have decided."

"Well said," Charles agreed, his eyes burning at his brothers. "It is the future of our sister we are discussing."

"And it being so, she has no reason for concern that right will be done by us, isn't that so, Charles?" Robroy asked.

"In a pig's eyes, Rob!" Charles snapped. "I will not listen to the pair of you." He turned to leave the room.

"Oh, Charles," Penelope pleaded, "stay, I beg you. I shall attend Marcus, but you stay and speak in my behalf."

He hesitated only a moment before nodding. "Of course, Pen. Otherwise these two will, with their poisonous tongues, convince Father that their own interests come above those of the rest of the world." His attention went to Marcus. "Marcus, my friend, take care that my sister is reassured while I make an end to the greed of my brothers."

"Come, Penny," Marcus said. "Your future is in good hands with two protectors such as these. Let us see this beautiful estate of the Rothschilds." With her hand on his arm, they stepped from the room.

No sooner had the door closed behind them than

Penelope clung to him, tears flowing from her eyes to wet the sleeve of his garment. "Oh, Marcus," she moaned, "how could they even voice such thoughts? How could anyone make such a demand as the baron has made?"

Placing his arm about her shoulders, he said, "Come, Penelope. There is little to concern yourself with. The days of giving children in marriage for such reasons are nearing a close. Come, show me these beautiful grounds."

Much later, while they sat in a garden alcove, Charles came from the house and called their names. When he'd been answered and made his way to their location, he gave his sister a weak smile and said, "It is settled, Pen, at least for today."

Her hand came to her mouth. "Oh, Charles, your manner doesn't console me. Could it be . . ."

"No. You are not yet condemned to life as a baroness. Father and I refused to allow such a thing."

"Then what is to be done about the Rothschild problem, brother?"

He shrugged. "The Rothschild fortunes shall, at the morrow's party, be no more, but we shall survive, Pen. Worry not of that." He turned to Marcus. "I wish sometimes that I could take this sister of mine and the earl to America, Marcus. It does seem, however, that I shall be hard put to make passage of my own. I doubt that I shall return with you, my friend."

"In truth, Charles, you do seem more content, in spite of all that's gone on, than you ever did in America," Marcus answered. "The passage, for you and also for the other Rothschilds who wish to go, is of no concern. If you so desire, we shall all make our way back to America."

Charles sent a glance around him before saying, "I truly had forgotten my love for this place, but my father would never leave his England. He will need my assistance if we Rothschilds are to survive in this world."

"What will we do, Charles?" Penelope asked sadly.

"Why, Pen, we will first leave Rothschild Halls. Then, the Lord willing, I will apply that which Marcus and America have taught me and procure a living for us."

"There is little in England which can be done as it is done in America," Marcus told him. "I suggest we give consideration to the problem of reacquiring the Rothschild fortunes from the baron."

They both looked at him as if he were mad. "And what can be done in that quarter, Marcus?" Charles asked. "You heard his demands. Never will we allow Pen to become the agent of our fortune's return."

"I did not suggest such, Charles," Marcus said. "I would spend some time alone, if I may."

"You surely cannot consider besting him at the gaming tables," Charles pressed. "I admit, Marcus, that you are on a point with the best in America, but to think that you could regain all that has been lost is lunacy. The man would see through the plot in an instant. He would not give you the opportunity for such a thing."

"The gaming tables were not in my mind, my friend. Now take your sister and leave me. I must think on the problem."

Penelope, her eyes full to the brim, crossed to him. "Marcus, it is of no concern to you. The problems of the Rothschilds are our own."

"Deny me not the pleasure of being a friend to those I admire, lass," he retorted. "Now, for once, mind me without argument. Go, both of you. Leave me to my thoughts."

After a moment's hesitation, the two departed, their voices low as they made their way across the lawn.

Behind them, Marcus got to his feet and managed

the crutch. Then, his mind working constantly, he re-traced the steps he had made in the company of Penelope. For some two hours, he walked thus, concentrating, shaking his head and finally saying aloud, "Ah, well, there is no help for it. So be it." With that, he made his way back to Rothschild Halls.

A manservant was at the door as he entered. Turning to the man, Marcus said, "I would closet with Charles. Do you know where I might find him?"

At that moment, Penelope came running from the dining room, her fists to her face, the tears coming freely. Without seeing him, she ran towards the staircase.

"My lady," Marcus called, "what is amiss?"

She stopped, her eyes meeting his. "Marcus . . . I . . . I have just spoken to Father. I shan't be ministering to you further. My thanks for all you've done for the Rothschilds. I shall never forget you." With that, she turned and ran up the stairs, her sobs ringing from the walls of the room.

"Oh, by all that's holy," Marcus said, working the crutch as fast as he could toward the dining room.

"Marcus," Charles called as he entered. "What—"

"Enough, Charles," the injured man snapped, his manner belligerent. "Am I to understand from your sister that the decision has been reversed and she is to become the wife of this Prussian?"

Charles's face fell. "Marcus, you actually—"

"The girl would have it no other way, friend Marcus," the earl stated. "Only moments ago, after holding her own counsel for some time, she came and insisted that her engagement to the baron be announced at the gala on the morrow."

"And you, sir, intend to allow this?"

"She gave neither her brother nor myself the moment to tell her we would not, sir," the earl protested.

"Marcus," Charles brought the man's attention to

himself. "Marcus, we will not allow her to do this thing. She has it seems, decided that she is to be the saving of the Rothschild fortune. That decision is not hers to make. Worry not, friend; we are not returned to the savage methods of former days."

Relief was obvious on Marcus's face at the revelation. A smile bent his lips. "Pray· go to your sister, Charles, and inform her that there may yet be a way to reacquire the Rothschild fortunes. Hurry, man, before she drowns in her own tears."

The statement brought both men to their feet. "What is it you say, Marcus?" Charles asked.

"You see a solution to our situation, sir?" the earl asked.

"I believe I do, my lord," Marcus answered. Then to Charles, "Go and speak to your sister. Relieve her mind."

Charles made as if to leave. Suddenly he turned back. "Marcus, if she is to be told any such thing, if such a thing can be true, she would much prefer to hear it from your lips than from mine." At a mild exclamation of curiosity from the earl, Charles faced him. "Father, I fear our Pen has been taken with my friend Marcus." He glanced at Marcus. "I further fear that he in turn has taken notice of her."

The earl stood silently for a long moment before saying, "Ah, that it could be so. Would that you were of the station necessary for such a thing, Marcus."

"Enough of that," Marcus said. "Charles, insist not on this tomfoolery."

Charles smiled knowingly. "Ah, but I do insist, Marcus. I concern myself not with your station and hers, only with her happiness . . . and yours. Will you tell us your thoughts?"

"I must beg a carriage for a trip to London," Marcus said. "I would speak with a solicitor."

"It is yours for the asking," the earl said. "But what of your plan?"

Briefly Marcus described the decision he'd come to while pacing the estate. When he'd finished, the earl shook his head.

"I cannot allow you to do it, sir. It is impossible to think such a thing. Even if it were to be allowed, he would refuse, and rightfully so. He is nobility and would not be bound by such a thing with you."

Marcus was about to speak when Charles said happily, "Ah, father, you cannot—"

"Prevent my attempting it," Marcus finished for him. "I am certain it will be as I have said. And the danger is nothing to concern yourself with."

"But your leg, Marcus," Charles protested. "It could well be the death of you."

"That will be disclosed eventually, will it not, Charles? If such is the case, so be it. But I think it won't come to that."

"Marcus, I cannot allow this," the earl said in finality. "The plan is as mad as the baron himself. I cannot hear of it."

"Then are you recalling your party invitation to me?" Marcus asked.

"Marcus, are you sure?" Charles asked. "You know what may be demanded?"

"I know, Charles. And yes, I am sure."

"Well then, Father," Charles said, "am I to understand that you, the head of the Rothschilds, intend to break your word to a man who has saved your daughter's life? Are you considering usurping the invitation you yourself made to this man?"

"Are you insane, Charles?" the earl asked, truly puzzled at his son's sudden change. "I cannot allow such a thing to take place."

"Father, if this is as Marcus desires, I myself feel he is entitled to this one small wish for the saving of my sister's life."

"But . . ." the earl began.

"And, Father, it would seem little enough for you to allow him to ease Pen's mind of the situation. He is, after all, sacrificing himself to danger for our benefit."

"I . . . I feel there is something here I don't understand," the old man said. His glance went from his son to Marcus. "However, since the two of you, for some reason or other, think it right, I accede. I repeat, though, Marcus, it is madness. He will not allow himself to be drawn in when there is no need."

"I would, since your son refuses, speak to your daughter, sir, and put her mind at ease."

The earl fixed him with an eye. "If it be true what this fun-seeking son of mine has said, I doubt that disclosure of your plans would ease her mind at all. Rather, I suppose she would be the more concerned."

"Your son—my friend—must have his joke, my lord. Truly, your Penelope has taken little notice of me."

"And you of her, sir?"

"She is a becoming lass, sir. I do, however, know my place."

"Very well. Speak with her. I warrant I know less of the goings on here than any of the three of you."

"Come with me, Charles," Marcus ordered.

"Gladly," the younger man said. As soon as they were out of the dining room, he asked, "Will it work, Marcus?"

Marcus shrugged. "With a bit of luck and cooperation from this damnable stick of wood, it has a chance, Charles. More I cannot promise."

"Well, you wished a carriage. I shall see to it. Go and speak with my sister. I shall call you when the carriage awaits."

"You were to come with me to your sister's chambers. Stop being such an ass and a matchmaker."

"The thought was yours that I accompany you, Marcus," his friend laughed. "I shall see to the carriage." With that, he stepped hurriedly to the front door and, still laughing, left the house.

"Blast!" Marcus said behind him. Then, a slight smile creasing his lips, he mounted the stairs.

CHAPTER SEVEN

He could hear her sobs when he reached the upper floor. Making his way forward, he came to an open chamber door and nearly ran into a disturbed Becky. "Oh, my lord," the maid said, "my apologies. My lady is in such condition, I pay no attention to where I go."

Placing a finger to his lips, he drew the girl to the hall, saying, "Go and get a cooling drink for your mistress. Take whatever time you can, as I would speak with her alone."

A light of understanding came into her eyes at the words. She smiled suddenly and nodded. "Aye, my lord, I think my mistress will shortly be her laughing self again. I shall take my time with the drink."

"Your imagination will have its way with you, will it not?" he asked. "Very well, for whatever reason you have conjured up, go for the drink."

A chuckle of secret knowledge escaped the girl's lips as she turned away from him and made her way down the hall.

"The chore of being unaware of the lass is made no easier by the persons surrounding her," he mumbled as he moved the crutch forward to enter the room.

She was lying on the bed, her face cradled in her arms, sobs racking her shoulders when he entered. She remained unaware of his presence until he bent to touch her hair and said, "Penny, my lass, stop this madness. Your good intentions are for naught. Neither your father nor your brother will allow you to wed the baron."

Her head came up to reveal tear-stained cheeks and puffy eyelids. "It is little enough for me to do to save my family, Marcus. There is no other way."

"There is a method, Penny. Believe me. The baron will not have his way with the Rothschilds if luck would be mine."

"There is nothing you can do, Marcus. It is left to me. I am what he desires and he will settle for no less." She dropped her head to her arms again. "Ah, that things could differ from what they are."

"Things are seldom as they seem, my Penelope. Now ease your mind. You shall not marry this oaf. And with luck, the fortunes of the Rothschilds shall be returned to their proper place. Come, let me see a smile before I leave."

Her head came up again. "You're leaving, Marcus? Why?"

"For only a moment. I return this same evening, late, and I shall breakfast with you on the morrow. Later I shall have the pleasure of viewing your loveliness at the gala in honor of your brother. Come— smile."

"I . . ."

"Smile for me, girl, so I might be about my business," he ordered with a chuckle.

She forced a smile in spite of herself, and he nodded. "That's better. Now go to your father and allow him to tell you of his concern for you. He is in need of your love." He assisted her from the bed and led her to the hallway and down the stairs. When they'd reached the lower floor he said, "I believe the earl is yet in the dining room. I will return shortly." Turning from her before she could question him further, he left the house to search for Charles and the carriage.

He found his friend in the carriage house talking to the hostler over a pint of grog. "Charles," he said from the doorway, "is this your usual method of preparing a carriage?"

Taken by surprise, the young man turned atop the cask upon which he sat and fell headlong onto the straw of the floor. His drink splashed out in front of him. Getting to his feet as Marcus laughed, Charles brushed at his clothing, saying, "That is an undue way for a friend to surprise one, Marcus. Come, I would have you meet Jolin, the best hostler in the business and the man who taught me what I know about horses. Jolin, meet the finest friend America ever offered."

When the two had shaken hands, Marcus turned to Charles. "I must make haste, Charles, if I'm to contact the solicitor."

"Fear not, friend. Jolin himself will drive us." He sighed heavily and added, "It is a terrible weight you've lifted from me this day, Marcus. Would you partake of a grog with me while the horses are being readied?"

Jolin, a man of strong hands and broad shoulders, said, "Aye, my lord; have a bit of it. There's none better. I'll have the animals ready in a sec." Turning, he left them.

"He's an old friend, Marcus," Charles said as he poured a tot of rum for both of them. "I'd nearly forgotten about him amidst all the problems." His smile broadened. "And did you ease the mind of my dear sister?"

"I did, my friend—and that's all. Now stop the prattle and let us go about doing what needs to be done."

"Will the sacrifice be such that you can make it,

Marcus? I have wondered if I have a right to ask such a thing of you out of friendship."

"Perhaps there will be no reason for the sacrifice, as you choose to term it, Charles," Marcus answered. "However, if the need arises, yes, I can make it. And not simply because we are friends. It strikes me that one way or the other, the baron would use his position and perhaps your brothers to secure Penny for his own. Besides, it is doubtful that any but us would consider such a thing a great sacrifice."

Charles nodded. "True, Marcus. They fail to know you as I do. They would consider it a dream come true for any man, I suppose."

The hostler returned with the horses and proceeded to a light carriage at the side of the barn. When the steeds were harnessed, he said, "Very well, my lords, what is your pleasure?"

Upon Marcus's departure, Penelope had at once made her way to the dining hall to speak with her father. He was as he had been when Marcus had left him, his face set in heavy lines of concentration, his thoughts consuming him.

"Father," she said softly, "Marcus has just left to go somewhere. Is it true, Father, that we can possibly salvage that which is lost?"

His eyes met hers and for a moment held them. Then he asked, "Do you think of this man as a friend, Penelope?"

"Why, of course, Father. And is he not a friend in your eyes?"

"Aye," the earl said with a nod. "Perhaps the dearest of friends. Certainly the most willing. But that is not what I had reference to, lass. Do you think of him in terms other than that of friend?"

She blushed heavily. "Father, how you do carry on! Do you think I am a starry-eyed dreamer?"

"No, certainly not that. But that is not an answer

to my question. Will you announce your feelings for this friend to me?"

The color deepened. She dropped her eyes from his. "Oh, Father, it is beyond explanation. He merely has to be within hearing distance for my blood to quicken. He is unlike any man I have ever met." She lifted her eyes. "I would love him if he would have me, Father, and follow him without a qualm wherever he traveled." She hesitated a moment, then asked, "Am I such a silly thing, Father?"

"Nay, not silly, Penelope," he answered sadly. "But, I fear, destined for heartbreak. He is a commoner; you are of the nobility; so it can never be, my child. Can't you see that?"

She nodded. "Yes, Father. He is a commoner and for that reason would never allow such a thing to happen. But were he to allow it, I would go off with him this instant, commoner or not."

A sadness entered the earl's eyes as he studied his daughter. "Ah, that your mother could be here to speak with you of this. That she could see the bloom which has, in so short a time around this man, come to your cheeks. Would that it were possible. The sacrifice you chose to make for your family becomes even greater in light of your feelings for him."

"And did you allow him to speak to me of that sacrifice, Father?"

He hesitated, his manner one of embarrassed confusion. Finally, when she'd begun to smile at him, he nodded, "Aye. Unseemly as such a thing is, I did allow it." His manner sharpened. "There's naught he did that was ill?"

She laughed outright. "No, Father, there was nothing. It pleases me to know that you would trust him to such an extent, though. What say you, Father? Let's all join him on his return to America."

He smiled shortly and opened his arms to her. "Ah, you will have your jest, will you not, daughter? But it cannot be. As he mentioned, he has a plan for returning the wealth of the Rothschilds to us. If his plan is successful, there would be no reason for any of us to leave our home."

Pulling back from him, she said, "Still, though he saves us from what has come, the idiocy of titles and proper places would prevent me having him if he should so desire."

The earl shrugged. "It is the manner of the world, my daughter. Would that I could give the man a title and make him wish your hand. But, alas, such is not possible."

She nodded. "Thank you, Father, for the thought." With obvious effort, she brought herself under control and asked, "And of this plan of his, Father. Will it succeed?"

"He told you of it?" the earl asked in disbelief.

"He told me nothing other than that I should forget my wedding the baron."

"He is correct. Had you but hesitated the fourth part of a second, your brother and I would have told you the same. We shall not allow anyone such as the baron to secure you in such a way. As to the plan put forth by Marcus, I myself can see no method for its success, things being as they are. He and your brother do, however, seem to have their own reasons for believing in its success. We shall see, since they insisted on the attempt."

Something in his tone caught her attention. "Is it a dangerous plan, then, Father? Is Marcus or Charles to be put in the face of danger for us?"

"I said nothing of danger," he muttered, refusing to meet her eyes. "Where you come up with such ideas is a mystery."

"You are not telling me the complete truth, Father. Tell me, please. I must know. Is Marcus to be placed in danger?"

"He himself has said the danger would be small,"

the earl hedged. "I doubt that he would make little of it if it were not so."

"You will tell me the plan, Father. You must." She put her arms around him and buried her head in his shoulder. "I love the man, Father. Though he may feel nothing for me, I love him. I must know what is about."

CHAPTER EIGHT

The carriage rocked with speed as it traveled through the darkness toward Rothschild Halls. Inside, Charles and Marcus sat quietly maintaining motion with the vehicle. Finally Charles broke the silence by asking, "The matter went well, Marcus?"

"For them, it did. Would that I could be as elated over such a thing as they. Ah, well, a man must do what he must. It's done and I must live with it."

Charles chuckled lightly. "I think there is less bitterness in you than I'd taken note of in America, my friend. In seriousness, tell me: Is my sister part of the reason for that?"

There was no answer for several turns of the carriage wheels. Then, when he was about to repeat the question, Marcus answered, "I find your sister attractive past the point of resistance, Charles. I do not, however, intend to press myself upon her."

"What? For God's sake, why not?"

"I am simply aware that she is too young yet to know her own mind about such things. She would do well to consider several men before she makes such a choice."

"You are mad. She is smitten with you. Lord, she would marry you in an instant."

"But she's still of an age where a lass has little but imagination to rule decisions concerning her emotions. No, Charles, it would not do. You shall not mention my words to her, either."

"But, Marcus . . ."

"Your word on it, my friend. Not a word of this to Penny."

Finally, with a nod unseen in the darkness, Charles said, "Very well, Marcus, but you do disappoint me. Would that I could call you my brother. Aye, that would be the day for rejoicing in the house of Rothschild."

"Your brothers would find it less appealing, I fear," Marcus chuckled.

"Those asses. If they but knew. Ho, when they realize, they will appear as toads."

"It might never become necessary for them to know," Marcus said. "If such is the case, then they are to remain ignorant."

"Of course. I do not find the faith in honor that you do, old friend. I fear the baron will have none of it unless it is beyond his powers to refuse."

"We shall see," Marcus said. "We shall see. My ankle tires of its labors this day. I hope it is not swollen again."

"Another poultice would be advised," Charles said. "I shall see to it immediately upon our arrival at the halls."

Rothschild Halls was dark when they drew to a stop at the front steps. With dragging feet, they got from the carriage and made their way up the steps. As they entered the door, a candle was lit in the library.

Penelope came from the room to meet them, her hair disheveled, her eyes giving testimony to her recent awakening. "Charles? Marcus?" she asked, nearing them. "Wherever have you two been?"

"On business," her brother assured her. "Why aren't you asleep?"

"I was concerned for both of you." Her glance shifted to Marcus. "I must speak with you, Marcus. I must."

"It is hardly the hour for a lady to be speaking to a gentleman who was but several days ago a stranger," he smiled. "Can it not wait until morning, Penny?"

She shook her head. "It must be now. It must. Father told me—"

"Oh, my lord," Charles moaned. "Father has allowed her to find out your plans, Marcus. Now there will be the devil's own time to pay before we are allowed to sleep."

She turned on him, saying, "To bed with you, Charles. It is with Marcus I speak."

"Only if you wish to do it in my chambers," Marcus said. "For I, dear lady, am going to bed." Working the crutch, he made his way past her toward the stairs.

"Very well, then," she said, "your chambers it will be. You cannot do such a thing as you have planned, Marcus. You cannot."

"It is settled, Penny," Charles told her. "Allow the man to sleep lest his weariness on the morrow causes him to misjudge."

The words halted her. For a moment she considered the man who was attempting to make his way up the stairs. Then suddenly she ran forward to help him. "Marcus, must it be this way? Must it?"

"Yes," he assured her. "I would have it no other way. Now, as your brother has said, I am tired. It might well be that I will need all my energy and wits about me on the morrow. I pray you, girl, go to your chambers and rest. It will be all right."

When they'd reached the head of the stairs, she stood looking up into his face for a moment before rising on tiptoe and placing her lips against his cheek. Then she was away from him and running toward her chambers.

"My sister has taken leave of her senses," Charles said. "Had Father been aware of such actions on her part, her backside would have known the leather."

Marcus stood staring after the girl. Finally, pulling himself back to the present, he said, "Your sister is as weary as we, my friend. She knows not what she is about. It was the embrace of a sister for a brother. You'll not mention it to your father, I trust."

Sighing loudly, Charles fixed his friend with a smile. "At this moment, I would promise anything for the feel of a soft bed against my body. Good night, friend. Sweet and pleasant dreams." He had taken two steps before he turned to ask, "Do you need assistance, my friend?"

"Nay," Marcus answered. "If need be, I shall sleep in my attire. A good night's rest to you, Charles." With that, he put the crutch into motion and made his way to his chambers.

Minutes later, having managed to remove his clothing, he fell upon the waiting bed and was instantly asleep. A smile was on his face as he slept, and many times his lips formed the name, "Penny."

Rothschild Halls was filled with the bustle and ado of party preparations when Penny awoke. Hardly had her eyes opened than she thought of what had transpired the night before. Hurrying from her bed, she called to Becky and managed her toilet. When she'd prepared herself for the morning, she stepped from her room and made her way down the hall, past Marcus's chambers, to the stairs.

The earl was at the dining table when she arrived, and his glance came up to meet hers as he smiled. "The day of reckoning for the Rothschild clan," he said.

She nodded, a concerned expression on her features. "You seem near happiness, Father. Has something occurred?"

He accepted her kiss on his cheek before saying, "There comes a time in an old man's life when he would simply have over with crisis. What God wills, will be, lass. There is nothing that can change it. One must accept what comes."

"You fear Marcus's plan will not succeed, Father?" she asked, taking a seat at the table.

"Were it as simple to perform as he says, it could hardly not succeed. I wish, however, that he would not attempt such a thing. There is the possibility that he overestimates his own abilities."

Her jawline stiffened. "If he determines it possible, I would hesitate to question him, Father. He does seem an extraordinary man. I'm sure Charles would agree."

The smile came to the old man's face again. "Love and comradeship have a means of accepting even the most fantastic endeavors, my child. But you are correct. He does seem an extraordinary person."

Breakfast was placed before her by a servant. When she'd taken several bites of the food, she said, "I awaited the return of him and Charles last night, Father. What was it they traveled to London in search of?"

He nodded. "I thought as much from your appearance. I would judge you slept little after their arrival."

"They would tell me nothing, Father. And Marcus would not listen to my pleas that he abandon this dangerous plan of his."

"Neither would they tell me of their reason for going to London. It seems we are both to be kept in the dark until the crucial hour. Do the preparations go to your satisfaction?"

She was surprised to realize that she had taken no

notice of the party preparations as she'd made her way to the dining room. "Truthfully, Father, I didn't notice. Since the announcement of the baron's demands, nothing has entered my mind other than the urgency of the situation."

He nodded sadly. "The mood in this house is less than desired for such a gala event as I'd planned for your brother's homecoming. Ah, well, at best it could have been only acceptable. Perhaps, by the end of this day, we shall have reason to rejoice."

"At what time will the baron arrive, Father?"

He shrugged. "Mid-afternoon, he informed me. He wishes to make an entry to impress all those who are present. The man is beyond belief."

"And am I to make the introductions of this Prussian devil to our friends and neighbors, Father?"

He shook his head. "No, girl. I would not ask that of you. I shall perform the service myself."

"And Rob and Monty, Father, will they arrive before or after the baron?"

A bitter laugh escaped his lips at the question. "Those two, I'll wager, will be among the first on hand. They would use the time to prepare a beggar's greeting for the Prussian, I imagine."

They became aware of voices outside the dining hall. The solid sound of crutch meeting floor punctuated the murmured words. Then Marcus and Charles entered the dining room and greeted the earl and Penelope.

"And did things go as you'd wished in London?" the earl asked when the two men had seated themselves.

"They did," Marcus answered. "It would seem we are to have a lovely day for the gala you've planned, my lord."

The earl nodded. "Which I take to mean you do not wish to discuss whatever it was that took the two of you from these halls last night. Very well, I will not press." His glance went to Penelope. "And my daughter shall not make a pest of herself with questions."

The girl reddened, but lifting her eyes to Marcus's face, she asked, "And did you sleep well, Marcus?"

"As a babe," he answered, smiling. "The night was full of pleasant dreams and much-needed rest."

"And your ankle, is it improved?"

"To the point that I look forward to casting this stick of wood away from me. And did you rest well, my lady?"

The servant brought the food at that moment, and Penelope returned to her eating without answering. Finally, as the two men began eating, she asked, "Can nothing make you change your mind, Marcus? We Rothschilds would not have you injured a second time in our behalf."

Charles smiled at her and said, "You have not the faith in our friend that he deserves, sister mine. Had you but watched him act before this, you would have little concern for his safety."

"But who has watched the baron? Who knows what he is capable of?" she demanded, her face coloring in anger at the attitude of her brother.

"He is capable of anything," Marcus said. "It is the anything I shall be on guard against."

Her color heightened at his words. "Oh . . . you make jest of my concern. The thoughts of conceited men do amaze me over much."

All three men laughed at her anger. Then, his voice soft, Marcus said, "I make no jest of you, Penny. I simply state matters as best I can. No one, neither I nor the baron, is infallible. However, the odds are with the person who judges himself in any position other than that of God."

"Enough of this talk," the earl said. "The day is one of festivity. Let us place smiles on our faces and prepare for the coming gala."

"As it should be," Charles agreed.

Penelope, about to speak again, looked to the faces of the three who shared the table with her and held her words. Finally it became too much for her and she got to her feet, saying, "Oh . . . men are a blight on the face of the earth!" Then she stomped from the dining room, leaving three amazed men in her wake.

"I think sister Pen is beside herself with concern," Charles said. "Perhaps I or you, Marcus, should go have a word with her."

"Remain where you are," the earl said. "The lass is upset, true. However, it is but a few hours till the midday beginning of the party. She will barely have time to attire herself before the hour, if I am to judge from recollection of her mother."

Both Marcus and Charles smiled at the statement. Then Charles fixed his friend with a questioning glance. "Marcus, would you attire yourself in a manner befitting you?"

"Exactly, my friend," Marcus answered with a smile. "I am a simple man. Therefore I shall dress simply. The wigs and silks of the court are for the childish."

"Harumph!" the earl coughed. " 'Tis the dress of fashion in this England you disparage, sir. And, while your America does not partake of such, I fancy they have practices of such a degree as ours."

"No offense, my lord. And you are correct in one respect but quite wrong in another. The practices of America are, in many cases, worse than those of England. The wigs and silks, however, are still a part of her people as they are of England's. It is only I who have no taste for such things."

The old man sat silently for a moment, his eyes studying Marcus as if to find a suggestion that he was being made sport of. When he'd satisfied himself that none such had been intended, he relaxed and turned to Charles. "And you, my son, will you powder and clothe yourself in the manner befitting your station?"

Charles shrugged. "I see no call for such a thing, Father. It is, I've found, more enjoyable at such a gathering if one is not burdened with the fancies of the court dandies. However, I will bow to your bidding."

"Your brothers shall arrive in splendor enough, I dare say. Perhaps it would appear more seemly if you were to dress according to your birthright."

"Very well, Father," Charles answered with a grimace at Marcus. "I shall do so. All who enter shall know that I am a proper son of Rothschild Halls." Pushing himself away from the table, he asked, "Marcus, would you partake of the tub before me or do you prefer to wait till later?"

Marcus, too, pushed himself back and reached for his crutch. "There is much I must see to in my chambers, Charles. Could you arrange for my large case to be brought to me? There are items within it I shall need. I must see to their care before the festivities begin."

"Immediately, Marcus," the younger man answered. "The case shall be brought to your room at once. And the tub shall be ready once you have completed your preparations. May I assist you on the stairs?"

"There is no need, friend. I seem to have the knack of this stick now. I shall manage." So saying, he got to his feet and, with a word to the earl, took his leave.

" 'Tis a brave man, he is," the earl said as Marcus left the room.

"And a good one, Father," his son added. "Well, I must see to his case. I trust we are all to be prepared to greet our guests at midday?" At the earl's nod, he left the dining room and called to a servant.

Attaining the head of the stairs, Marcus moved toward his room and was at the doorway when Pe-

nelope called his name. Turning, he faced the girl,
who stepped quickly toward him, a peignoir covering
her and a scolding Becky in her wake.

"It is unseemly, ma'am," the maid said. "What will
the earl think of such actions as this?"

"Oh, bother," Penelope snapped over a shoulder.
"I am more covered as I am than are you in your
low-bodice gown, Becky. I doubt that Marcus will
find it shocking." Then she was near him, her eyes
resting on his face.

"My lady," he said, smiling at the change in the
girl's mood.

"Marcus, you must decide for me," she began in a
breath. "Shall I wear the blue silk you know, or would
you prefer I wear something more . . . more . . ."
Color suddenly swept into her face and she dropped
her eyes from his. "It seems I am ever the fool where
you are concerned, Marcus," she finished lamely.

"My lady," Becky exclaimed. "Allow me to take
you to your chambers. This is unseemly."

"Enough, Becky," Marcus said. "Your mistress is
correct. Her attire does not shock me, nor is there a
reason it should. She bares nothing save her arms and
neck." He paused, then reached to place a finger under
Penelope's chin. When he'd lifted her head until her
eyes met his, he said, "If you truly wish my decision,
Penny, I would like you to wear something other
than the blue silk. The dress is beautiful, but it truly
does lack something you require and I prefer."

The meaning she read into his words brought a
smile of happiness to her features. She spun around,
nearly knocking Becky aside in her haste to return
to her chambers. "Thank you, Marcus," she called
over her shoulder. "Come, Becky, the red velvet.
Hurry."

With a glance at Marcus, Becky said, "Your concern
over the exposure of her bosom has pleased her beyond words, my lord. It is my thanks I offer you for

the relief you bring her in these pressing times."

"Go see to her needs, Becky," Marcus said, turning to his chambers. "You are truly all the relief your mistress needs."

Only minutes after Marcus had entered the room, there came a rap on the door. Moving to open the portal, he was greeted by Charles, who stood in the fore of two servants bearing the large wooden chest containing his belongings.

"It occurred to me, Marcus, that you might require assistance in opening the chest. While you do balance well on the crutch, the bending necessary to remove the contents might be too much for you."

Marcus nodded in approval of his friend's consideration. "You are probably correct. Should I attempt to stand on my head to reach the contents, I shall surely end up encased within my own baggage." He stepped aside to allow the servants to enter with the chest. When he and Charles were alone in the room, he said, "The item I seek is midway through the packing, Charles. You remember it well, I'm sure."

"That I do," Charles answered, opening the chest and removing items of clothing. It was some minutes later when he muttered a sound of discovery and lifted a gold-chased wooden case from the chest. Turning to Marcus, he asked, "Would you like me to prepare them for you, Marcus?"

"I shall see to it, my friend. As you will recall, it is something I would trust to no hand save my own. Place them on the bed, if you will."

When he'd done as asked, Charles turned, saying, "I shall be in my chambers if you need me for anything. Until then, I shall prepare myself for the coming festivities." Turning, he left the room, pulling the door closed behind him.

Once he was alone in the room, Marcus crossed to the bed and snapped the catches on the wooden case.

Lifting the lid, he removed the matched pair of gold-inlaid dueling pistols from their protective velvet bed and hefted them. For several seconds, he held the pieces in memory of days past. Then, removing materials from the case, he began methodically to prepare the weapons for their job.

CHAPTER NINE

Penelope was resplendent in her high-necked, red-velvet gown and coiffured hair when she descended the staircase at midday. Below her at the foot of the stair stood Marcus, the earl, Charles and, off to one side, Robroy and Montgomery. Her eyes were steady on Marcus's face as she progressed one step at a time toward him. Her heart skipped a beat when his eyes found her and widened in pleasant surprise; the smile which formed on his lips was the approval she had hoped for and more.

His was the first hand to be extended to her as she managed the final step. Bowing, he murmured, "My lady, you do take the breath away from one such as I. Never has there been one as lovely in my presence."

His words filled her with a pleasure she had never before known. She was aware of the heat of color in her face but did not concern herself with it. "I think you are afflicted with sudden blindness, Marcus," she murmured in answer. "Either that or you elect to make jest with me."

"Blindness it is," he returned, meeting her gleaming eyes, "brought on by the sight of yourself, my lady."

"Enough of that, Penelope," Robroy snarled. "Must you make over the commoner so? It seems the saving of one's life has the power required to remove all inhibitions and signs of decent upbringing. You disgrace your family before their very eyes."

"And a good day to you, also, brother Robroy," she answered caustically. "My, I see you have chosen the white brocade to impress the Prussian fool. No dandy of the court has ever appeared as foppish."

Robroy grimaced at her words and took a step forward, only to be intercepted by Charles. "Hold your temper, Rob, lest I introduce you to the crudity of America."

The heir of the Rothschilds met his brother's eyes for a long moment, read something there and turned away with an oath. To Montgomery, who stood as if tasting something uncommonly bad, he said, "It would appear it is for us to uphold the pride of the Rothschild name, brother. Our sister and brother and, aye, even our father seem bent on lowering themselves to the level of the commoner. Come, let us greet the invited as they should be greeted to the halls."

"Fools," Penelope muttered when the two had left the house for the porch. "Father, must we allow them to make us appear as fops?"

The earl chuckled lightly at her protest. "They will seem such only to you, Penelope, my child, for they will be greeting those who are of much the same mind about things." His glance shifted to Marcus. "I will not knowingly allow any to bear you insult, sir. It is, I fear, a possibility that cannot be ignored. I apologize for any actions taken here today against you."

Charles burst into laughter at the statement, only to cease suddenly when Marcus's glance fell on him.

"Have no fear, my lord," Marcus answered the earl. "Words have little effect on me. I fear it is one of the

shortcomings they speak of when using my name."
He was interrupted by the sound of a coach arriving at
the outer steps.

"Oh, Lord," Charles exclaimed peering out. "Hide
the maids and all other females. It is the ancient
Viscount of Ferrel. Be glad you are wearing a gown
such as you are, Penelope."

"Enough, Charles," the earl protested. "The viscount's habits are well known throughout the kingdom. There is little need to call attention to them."

At mention of the visitor's name, Marcus's lips had
thinned to a straight line. Beside him, Penelope took
notice of the change in his expression and asked, "Is
something troubling you, Marcus?"

Charles looked to his friend at her words. His eyes
widened in understanding and he looked to the
heavens in silent prayer. Then the viscount was entering the doorway and offering his hand to all and
sundry.

"My Lord Rothschild," he said, nearly losing his
balance at the threshold, "it was with pleasure I re-
ceived your invitation. My thanks to you and yours."
His eyes went to Charles and he squinted slightly.
"Ah, and this must of necessity be young Charles.
How are you, my boy?"

"As well as can be," Charles answered. "And your
health, sir?"

"Extremely well for my years, Charles. Had enough
of the foreign flag, have you?"

"For the present, sir," Charles told him. But the
man had already turned away to Penelope. The old
eyes widened when they lit on the girl and a smile of
pure lechery captured the man's wrinkled lips. He
moved unsteadily toward her, his hand extended in
readiness to capture hers. "And my lovely Penelope,"
he said, grasping her hand.

"My lord," she said, resisting his effort to pull her
to him. Dropping into a curtsy, she tugged her hand

free of his and smiled. "We are pleased at your presence, my lord." She turned to indicate Marcus. "May I present a friend of the Rothschilds, Mr. Marcus Manners."

Reluctantly the viscount tore his eyes from her and placed them on Marcus. For a moment, he stood without moving, as if reading every pore in the face of the stranger. Then he said, quite to himself, "No, that is not the name. Jove, what is it?"

"Sir?" Penelope asked. "You missed his name, did you? It is Manners, my lord. He is a friend of the family Rothschild."

Finally the old man accepted the hand offered by Marcus. His eyes were locked on the face of the younger man as their hands touched. "No, that's not the name," he mumbled again.

"Come, my friend," the earl said, taking the arm of the older man, "let's proceed to the tables and have some wine before the festivities begin."

"Eh? Oh, yes," was the answer. "Not the name at all," he mumbled as the earl led him away.

"He becomes doddering since the death of his lady," Penelope said, with a smile at Marcus. "He thought you to be someone else. It is embarrassing, but excusable in one such as he."

Charles stepped forward to say, "If our brothers choose to be asses and greet all on the step, so be it. It occurs to me that we have servants to announce guests in a manner befitting their rank. Come, both of you, let us join Father and the viscount. I would sip the wine."

"And I," Penelope agreed. "It will be only a short while before the ladies of our brothers appear in all their giddiness, and that is truly enough to sicken one."

Marcus laughed at the girl's words. "Are they then as bad as you suggest, Penny?"

"Much worse, Marcus," Charles assured him before

Penelope could answer. "They are the prudes of the kingdom. It will be worth much to note the expressions on their faces later in the day when—"

"Your tongue seems loose at both ends," Marcus said. "Until the moment necessity should require, let us remain silent."

Curiosity plain on her features, Penelope looked from her brother to the man she so loved. "Now what is it you two have afoot that is of such secrecy?"

Charles sobered. "Nothing to concern you, lass. If need be, you shall learn of it soon enough."

Her glance was on Marcus. "What is it, Marcus? Tell me, for I cannot abide secrets."

"As Charles has said, my lady, it is nothing. Nothing, at least, that I care to have known unless called for."

She would have persisted had it not been for the servant calling the titles and names of new arrivals to the halls. With a scornful look at both her male companions, she said, "I fear I must act as lady of the halls, my secretive gentlemen. By your leave." She removed her hands from their arms and turned to welcome the guests.

Marcus sighed and fixed his friend with a look of intentness. "Let not the wine loosen your tongue, Charles. I would that no more than necessary be brought to light."

"As you will, Marcus. It does strike me as humorous that the old fool of a viscount is in a quandary about you."

"Let him be, Charles," Marcus said as they entered the great dining hall and accepted drinks from a servant.

Well into the afternoon, when all present were enjoying the day of rest, the musicians began to play. Marcus, standing by himself along one side of the dining hall, watched the couples leave the large table of food and drink one after another to make their way to the room of melody. It was shortly after the music began that he noted two newly arrived ladies enter and send searching gazes around the persons remaining in the dining room. A chuckle rose to his lips at sight of the two, for they were extremely different from one another. One was of a height less than five feet and weighed in excess of two hundred pounds. Her face was rouged to excess and her coiffured hair stood perilously high above her head. The other was of a height nearing Marcus's own six feet and weighed not more than a hundred and twenty pounds. The outstanding feature about her was the overlarge bosom that seemed to threaten her balance. The chuckle within him grew until his shoulders were shaking. Then he saw that Penelope had the two ladies in tow and was crossing the room toward him.

There was no place for him to turn, much as he desired to conceal himself from the two. With an effort, he controlled his laughter as they came before him.

"Marcus," Penelope said, a glow of impishness in her eyes, "may I present the ladies Rothschild. "Mildred," she indicated the tall one, "and Constance. Ladies, a friend of the Rothschilds, Marcus Manners."

The tall one aimed her nose at him and sighted down it. "Are you of the court, my lord?" she asked, her voice reedy.

"No, not I," Marcus answered, noting the humor floating in Penelope's face. "It is a commoner I am, my lady. Titles bore me."

The effect on the two was immediate. Their mouths dropped, their eyes widened and both of them swung to fix Penelope with an irate stare. As suddenly as they'd come, they turned from Marcus and, with noses in the air, left him.

The rear view of the two crossing the great hall

was too much for Marcus. The laughter he'd been holding had its way, and he guffawed loudly.

"For shame, Marcus," Penelope said. "Now you have insulted my sisters-in-law." Then she, too, was laughing.

"It's truly a fair sight they make," Marcus got out when he'd controlled himself somewhat. "Would that such a sight could be preserved for the future members of the world."

"Prigs," she answered, gasping for breath. "They'll go now to their husbands and bend their ears for an hour over the commoner who was so brash as to barge into the festivities."

"It is of no . . ." He ceased talking as the servant in the doorway called the name of Baron Von Lentin, late of the Prussian guard.

A shudder wiped all humor from Penelope's body at the announcement of the name. She turned, her eyes going to the entryway. "He is here, Marcus," she murmured as if in fear to speak aloud.

"And, I presume, as Prussian as can be expected," he answered, taking her arm. "Shall we?"

Her hand tightened on his arm and she sighed, "Please, Marcus, don't do anything. I beg you. It is of no consequence that the Rothschilds are in straits. You must not risk injury to yourself."

"Come, my lady," he said, ignoring her plea. "The earl will expect us to greet the baron." Placing her hand on his arm, he made their way toward the man who had just entered. "Fancies himself a dandy," he murmured, taking in the obesity of the man, and the red-and-white silken knee britches he wore.

The earl left the group with which he had been conversing at the call of the baron's name. As he approached to greet the man, the Prussian fixed him with a condescending eye and, in a loud voice, said, "Ah, yes, Rothschild Halls. It is as I recall. I find your taste boring, Earl."

The earl reddened under the attack. Holding his temper in check, he said, "Baron, welcome to Rothschild Halls. Would you care for some wine?"

"I doubt that your wine will suit a taste such as mine," was the answer, again loud enough for even the dancers in the other room to hear.

The music died as the dancers, caught by the tenor of the voices, abandoned their pleasure and returned to the main dining hall.

"If the baron would, there are those who would make your acquaintance," the earl sputtered, covering his embarrassment.

An expression of complete disgust was on the Prussian's face as he said, "Oh, very well, if we must. Bring your stupid sons before me that I may see them. And, of course, the daughter whom you will, I'm sure, present in the proper manner, for your guests' ears."

"The daughter first, baron," Rothschild said, turning to take Penelope's hand as she and Marcus approached. "Baron, my daughter, Penelope. Penelope, you recall the baron Von Lentin, do you not?"

"I do, Father," she answered, retaining her hold on Marcus's arm, making no move to curtsy.

The Prussian eyed her for a long moment before shifting his gaze to Marcus. His eyes narrowed as he detected the hint of a smile on that face. "And, Rothschild, who is this who escorts my lady to me?"

"One who has little use for Prussian offal," Marcus said. Removing Penelope's hand from his arm, he said to her, "Go, little lass, away from this mound of garbage else you become infected by the stench of such."

The entire hall was silent as if holding one monstrous breath. The two eldest sons of Rothschild stood about to enter the hall, their mouths agape, their eyes bulging.

The baron's eyes had widened at the words of the stranger. Anger swept all other emotion from his face as he swung to face the earl. "If this man be a friend of yours, he acts it not," he snarled.

"If you wish to say something to me, Baron," Marcus said, the smile still playing at his lips, "face me. I will brook nothing from a Prussian coward. Though I am told there is nothing else in that lowly kingdom."

"May I present Marcus Manners, Baron Von Lentin," the earl said in the silence which followed the statement.

"Rothschild, I shall . . ." the baron exploded.

"Hold, heavy belly," Marcus said, gripping the arm of the man. "Speak not to Rothschild. If you have a complaint, sir, then make it to the proper quarter. If, indeed, you have the stomach to do so."

Suddenly the baron jerked free of Marcus's grip. His hand came around to slap the cheek of the man who had borne him nothing but insult. "I shall kill you for those words," he said as Marcus's head turned under the impact of the blow.

When Marcus again brought his eyes to meet the baron's, the smile was still on his lips. He bowed as best his crutch would allow. "Your servant, sir. I believe the choice of weapons is mine."

The smile remained an enigmatic threat. The Prussian's glance went to Rothschild, who stood as a statue watching the procedure. The glance moved around the gathering and finally came back to rest on Marcus's face. "I heard no title before your name, sir. I would not lower myself to duel a commoner."

Again Marcus bowed, "I choose pistols, Baron. Shall we say at sunrise, on the morrow?"

"Have you no sense of hearing, you peasant?" the baron breathed. "I will not fight one of your station. It would not be seemly."

"Ah, and when has a Prussian concerned himself about such as that, my lord?" Marcus asked, the smile broadening.

"Enough. I have stated my position. I shall have a servant do for you."

"No, not a servant, sir," Marcus protested. "You have no choice but to do the thing yourself."

"No choice," Von Lentin growled in genuine disbelief. "I am of the nobility. I have no cause to soil my hands on such as you. You will hear from my man on the morrow." He turned from the smiling face toward Rothschild. "I fear you have—"

"Hold, sir," Marcus said, clutching the man's arm and turning him back. "You will not duel those of a lesser rank than yourself, you say. I understand your reluctance. Of course, there is none of rank lesser than yourself, even in Prussia. Will you then, my lord, take up arms against a duke?"

Charles chose that moment to step forward amid the confusion caused by the question. In his eyes was a gleam that was bested only by the smile on his face. "Baron Von Lentin, may I present my good friend and comrade, Lord Marcus Mantique, Duke of Barrington."

"That is the name. That is the name," the Viscount of Ferrel mumbled aloud as he tottered forward to look into Marcus's face, unaware of what had passed. "Of course it is. Now I recall." He would have dropped to a knee had not Marcus caught him.

"Yours is not for that, old friend," Marcus told him. "Stand. It is happy I am to see you."

"My lord," the old man said, "you've grown into a man your father would have been proud of. But why did you abandon the dukedom?"

"Later, friend," Marcus said. "I would have words with the baron."

The old man turned to squint at the Prussian. For a moment he held the angry, disbelieving eyes of the man, then he turned again to Marcus. "You fell from my knee at one time, Marcus."

"Later, please," Marcus repeated, steering the old man to Rothschild. "Now, Baron, shall we say sunrise on the morrow?"

It seemed the Prussian would be unable to find words. Finally, with a bitter glance around the assemblage, he nodded shortly. "Sunrise, on the morrow, at the Glen of Finrose. It is my duty, Duke, to inform you that I am an expert shot."

"As am I," Marcus said.

"Harumph," the man coughed. "I'll have no more of these surroundings." His glance went to Rothschild. "Nothing has changed, Rothschild. On the morrow, I shall do away with this Duke of Barrington and then your debt will be due."

"Hold," Marcus called. "My friend Rothschild tells me you are a gambling man, my lord. Would a wager on the morrow's sport tempt you?"

"Wager on a duel?" the baron demanded. "Are you mad?"

"Are you so afraid that you will not?" Marcus shot back.

The Prussian was silent for a long moment before asking, "And what was it you were of a mind to wager?"

"The property and fortunes you hold of the Rothschilds," Marcus answered, without hesitation.

"You jest," Von Lentin snarled. "You would match the worth of such as that?"

Marcus shook his head. "No, my lord, not match it; best it. I stand prepared to wager the dukedom of Barrington and all that is implied by such against that which you hold over the Rothschild head. Is Prussian courage worthy of such a wager, or is it, as I suspect, only idle gossip that makes such claims?"

Anger flooded over the Prussian, and his breath came heavily as he stared at the brash young man before him.

"Well, my lord, do we have a wager, or do you freely admit before all here that you are of no stomach for such a thing?" Marcus asked.

"You have a wager, my foolish Englishman," the baron growled. "Yours will be the residence of myself and my bride."

"And, my lord," Marcus continued, ignoring the threat, "would you that the first blood drawn is an end to the thing?"

"I shall kill you," Von Lentin snarled.

"So be it, then. A paper concerning the wager will be necessary," Marcus said. He turned away from the man and sought Penelope. Behind him, the baron growled deep in his throat and turned to stomp from the halls, thrusting his weight against any who barred his way.

As suddenly as it had fallen, the silence over the dining hall ended. From all sides could be heard the word "duke," spoken in amazement. Robroy and Montgomery moved forward from a paralysis-like stance to stand before Marcus.

"My lord," Robroy said, dropping to a knee, "had I but known . . ."

"Out of my way, you ignorant dandies," Marcus ordered. "Take yourselves and your foolish ladies from my sight, else I shall present you as a gift to the baron when I have managed him on the morrow. Move, I say."

"But, my lord . . ." Montgomery began.

"Enough of your groveling," Rothschild said, coming to stand beside Marcus. "Leave, as you've been told. And take your ladies with you. Even now they descend upon his lordship. Stop the sniveling witches."

Immediately the two men rose and hurried to head off their wives.

"My thanks, my lord," Marcus said.

The earl met the glance of the newly announced

duke and bowed from the waist. "I am as my sons, your lordship. Had I but known . . ."

"You could hardly have appeared a more perfect host, my lord." His eyes swept around the room. "Have you seen Penny, my lord?"

Rothschild smiled broadly, "My lord, she was on the arm of my son Charles when last my eyes beheld her. His arm was needed, I fear, for you have taken the lot of us by surprise. Your tale is but rumor to me, but I recall it well."

"It is nothing, my lord," Marcus said impatiently, his eyes moving constantly around the hall. Then, as an opening appeared in the crowd, he spied Penelope and Charles sitting on a sofa at the side of the room. "By your leave, my lord," he said to the earl, "I would speak with your daughter."

"Of a certainty, my lord Duke," the earl answered. "I only—"

"No title, if you please," Marcus asked. "I truly prefer the name Marcus."

Rothschild bowed. "As you please, Marcus. Go now and speak with Penelope. I think her shock is greater than any, her sentiments being as they are."

Marcus took a step away from him and turned back. "My Lord Rothschild, it occurs to me that should I survive tomorrow's encounter, I shall, when she has had time to become of a logical mind, speak to you of Penny."

The expression on the earl's face became animated. "Oh, my lord, you do this house and the Rothschilds an honor."

"Enough," Marcus said. "She is yet a child. When she has had suitable time to decide for herself, we shall speak further." Turning, he made his way through the throng to where Penelope and Charles sat.

Charles met his glance and smiled broadly. "My sister is overcome, Marcus," he laughed. "Whether by the tension of the moment or the revelation, I know not."

At mention of the name, Penelope's head came up. Her eyes met the blue ones and she came from the couch to drop into full curtsy before Marcus. "My lord," she murmured, "had I but known, I—"

"Ah, sister mine," Charles laughed, "how is it you are suddenly impressed by titles?"

"Enough, Charles," Marcus ordered, bending to touch the girl's hair. "Never before me again, Penny. Never. Raise yourself. I would have you on my arm for the extent of this gala."

"My lord, I—"

"It is the same Marcus as it was but a short while ago, lass. Now, on your feet. Else I shall have to bend you over my knee and use this infernal crutch on your backside."

Coming to her feet, she reluctantly met his eyes. "Did you choose to make sport of us, Marcus?"

"No, Penny. The revelation, had there been a choice, would not have been made. I have no use or desire for the dukedom." He paused and presented his arm to her. "Will you have my arm, my lady?"

She sent one happy look at her brother before placing her hand upon Marcus's arm and saying, "Happily, my lord Marcus. I am yours to command."

"And I command for the final time that you cease using title when you speak to me. My, but you are the stubborn one."

Her expression sobered suddenly. "Marcus, he stated that he was an expert pistol shot. What if—"

"Every man who duels and lives fancies himself an expert, Penelope. And, to an extent, they are correct until they no longer live. Worry your head not about the morrow. It will as it will. There's none to change it now. Come, let us join the festivities."

"I think you will tire of the attention afforded you, Marcus," Charles offered with a glance around them.

"Observe. Even now they await you. Can you withstand such offerings as these and still hold down your meal?"

Marcus grimaced at the words. Sending a cautious glance around himself, he muttered, to the delight of Charles and Penelope, "The animals had not growled in such a time, I'd forgotten them. Would that I could absent myself. Ah, well, the doing is my own. So be it. Let us join your father."

"Would that you could dance with the assistance of the crutch, Marcus," Penelope said. "I have a feeling you would shame all others on the floor."

"Aye, that he would, Pen," Charles told her. "There is none as light as Marcus in the dance."

"My lord," came a shaky voice from behind Marcus. Turning, Marcus nodded to the Viscount of Ferrel. "Ah, old friend, and do the days treat you well?"

A smile of pleasure broke the face of the old man. He cocked his head to the side and winked. "And the citizenry, Marcus. They make jest of my doddering ways and say naught when I do as I will with the ladies."

Marcus threw back his head and laughed heartily at the words. Behind him, he heard first the gasp and then the laughter of Penelope as she came to his side. "My lord," she said to the viscount in a scolding manner, "from this moment forward, you shall not get near me. I, as others, had thought you senile."

"Hush, lass," the old man ordered, "lest those ladies of ample proportion hear your words and do away with the only pleasure an old man has remaining." He returned his attention to Marcus. "Would that I might speak with you, Marcus. There is much I would ask you of the several years since your father's passing."

Marcus glanced over the crowd, searching for a route through the throng. Charles was beside him. "Come, Marcus," he said, "I think your ankle is bothering you over much. I shall find private chambers for you." So saying, he stepped into the crowd, announcing that the duke was tired because of his injury and needed rest. Hard on his heels came Penelope, the viscount and Marcus. Ladies curtsied and gentlemen bowed to Marcus as the four made their way from the dining hall.

When they had closeted themselves in Marcus's chambers, Charles said, "I shall leave you now. Please allow me a moment to inform Father of what is to pass. He would, I'm certain, desire to know the truth of what has come about this day. He was in as much amazement as the rest of the hall."

Marcus nodded. "Inform the earl that I am at his service and shall return to his gala shortly, should he desire to remain with the invited."

"Tell Father I am with Marcus, Charles," Penelope said. "I, too, would like to hear the tale of what has been revealed this day."

Charles took his leave, and for several minutes, the viscount and Marcus were involved in discussion of other times. Shortly, the earl entered the room, saying, "My lord, Charles has said that you would disclose that of your past which has this day amazed our gathering and brought honor to Rothschild Halls. Would that I could be privy to such an explanation."

"Seat yourself, my lord," Marcus said, glancing around for a chair. Then, before he could speak again, Penelope got up from her chair and gave it to her father. With only a glance in her father's direction, she approached the bed where Marcus sat, asking, "Marcus, might I sit upon the edge of the bed, as do you?"

"As you will, Penny," he answered, moving to the side for her to sit.

"Well done," the viscount cackled. "Best you watch him most carefully, Penelope. The old duke was a rake if ever there was such, and from the looks of this son of his, it is a thing which has been passed."

She colored at the statement and dropped her glance.

"Well, Marcus," the viscount asked, "what of your sudden departure from the dukedom? Why would any do such a thing? And where did you hie yourself? All England was aware of your departure from Barrington, and for days, until your solicitors made the announcement, you were feared dead."

Marcus nodded. "For that I am sorry. There were those of you who loved me not because of the dukedom but for myself. The concern I afforded you is heavy on me yet."

"We were much relieved when we heard from your solicitor, Marcus. But I detain you. Tell us what it is you have been involving yourself with these many years."

With a smile at Penelope, Marcus said, "It is, I fear, a tale of one who could not bear the responsibility of a title, nor the foppishness which attended it. Upon my father's death, I, at an age younger than Penny, became the lord of all that is Barrington. I fear my youth was such that I seemed an apt target for all who would partake of whatever they could. In my twentieth year, it occurred to me that I should, lest I be constantly wary, forgo all that my father had toiled his many years to amass. It was then I decided to absent myself from this England. I contacted my solicitors, and within a matter of days, we had arrived at a method whereby the dukedom would be managed by the solicitor's firm and held in readiness should I desire to return to it. Within a fortnight of that time, I boarded a ship bound for America. The name Marcus Manners has been mine for those seven years, and I have indeed become less responsible to the titled nobility than at the time I departed. It was only of necessity that the disclosure was made today. I had hoped it would not be so."

"And in this America," the viscount asked, "what was it you found there to occupy yourself, Marcus?"

Marcus shrugged. "There is much, old friend. I have served as a paid hunter, a boatman, a gambler and whatever else turned its attention to me. I have learned much and have prospered. It is a raw, wealthy country full of promise for those who have the courage to face it."

"And in this seven years, Marcus, have you taken a wife?" the old man asked, his glance going to Penelope.

She laughed lightly at the suggestion and asked, "Aye, Marcus, have you wife and children my brother neglected to mention? I think not, for Charles would not have allowed . . ."

"Yes, my lady?" Marcus asked as she faltered.

"I was about to say," she continued, blushing, "Charles would not have neglected to mention your family to Father, had you had such a thing."

"Tell me, Marcus," the viscount asked, "is your handling of pistols such that you can look safely to the morrow? For I have witnessed the baron's skill on the dueling ground. He is quick and sure when snapping the flint."

Marcus shrugged. "Until the morrow, there is none can say who will be best. God's will, will out. Other than that, there is nothing to do but wait."

"Your ankle," Penelope exclaimed. "Will it cause you discomfort to the point of endangering your life?"

"No," he assured her. "I think that with the assistance of a poultice, by morning I shall stand without the crutch for long enough to complete this business."

"The sacrifice you attempt for the Rothschilds is beyond any expectation one should have of a friend," Rothschild murmured. "The house of Rothschild, whatever it may become, is to be in your debt forever."

"Enough," Marcus said. "The festivities are below. I would indeed rest my ankle and contemplate my actions for the morrow."

As the earl and the viscount rose to leave, the viscount asked, "And is it your father's pistols you shall use on the morrow, Marcus?"

"It is," Marcus answered. "Fine weapons."

"And touched with a bit of luck, as I recall, my friend. May God go with you to the dueling site." With that, he followed the earl from the chambers.

"You miss the gala, Penny," he said when the two men had gone.

She shook her head. "I don't miss the dandies and their ladies. Their antics bore me to the extreme. Would that I might sit with you for a while, if I may."

"It is a poultice I am in need of this day, Penny. A poultice and a goblet of the fine wine your father serves below."

"Immediately, my . . . Marcus," she said. "I shall return with all haste."

When she'd returned and applied the poultice, she again left and shortly returned with two goblets of wine. Passing one of them to him, she said, "I fear for your safety on the morrow, Marcus." She sipped at the wine and added, "To risk one's life in such a way appears utter nonsense."

He nodded. "Nonsense it truly is, Penny. But such is the method of society. Ah, that men could love life enough that such things would be brought to an end. But don't concern yourself. I shall survive."

"And should you return the Rothschild fortunes by your bravery, what then? Tell me, Marcus, what plans do you have beyond the morrow?"

He was thoughtful for only a moment. "It had been my intent to return to America at the soonest possible moment. Now, however, having again set foot in England and having taken steps I had not planned, I am in a quandary. The decision will have to wait until the business of the morrow is settled."

Suddenly her eyes clouded. "Marcus, I . . ." she began, then she stood and ran from the room. Behind her, Marcus sat in complete surprise.

After several moments, he tipped the goblet to his lips and downed the wine. "Ah," he said as he lowered the vessel, "she is as caring a lass as any man would deem proud to call his own." With that thought in mind, he placed the tankard beside the bed and, with a sigh, rolled to a comfortable position and fell asleep.

He was unaware of her return to the room an hour later. She entered, crossed to the foot of the bed and stood staring down at him. Her eyes were red from weeping. And suddenly they again filled and she turned to make her way from the room. "Live, Marcus, please, for me," she murmured as she stepped from the chambers and softly pulled the door closed behind her.

CHAPTER TEN

Marcus arose well before dawn and attended to his toilet. That done, he moved the candle to the table, withdrew paper from his luggage and applied quill to it. He finished shortly and, using the crutch, made his way to the lower level of Rothschild Halls.

Charles was about when he entered the dining room. The younger man turned to fix his friend with a glance of evaluation. "And what of your feelings this morn, Marcus?"

"They remain as they were, Charles. I neglect myself. I seem to be without second for this day's chore." He shook his head. "Perhaps you were correct. It is old I am getting. It did completely slip my mind yesterday."

Charles smiled. "And who other than myself would you have for second, Marcus? It is assumed; I shall second you. Father is even now preparing to attend the meeting. And, I am certain, my brothers and several of those present yesterday shall attend. There shall be witnesses enough to whatever passes, Marcus. Fear not."

"The fear is there as always. It is a foolish man who faces death with no touch of fear in him. I may indeed be getting older, yet I hope I am not foolish."

"Would you have breakfast before the meeting, Marcus?"

"That will wait, my friend. Let us to the agreed site. I shall get the weapons and return."

Charles was moving toward the door. "I shall get the case for you, Marcus. Rest easy till I return." He was gone, and in but a few minutes returned with the pistol case. "I fear Penelope is awake," he announced.

"Then let us be gone. There is nothing for her to do, and I would have my mind free of any thoughts not of this business."

"Of course, my friend. Let us away. Father will follow in his own carriage."

The short trip to the dueling site was a silent one. When the carriage pulled to a stop, Charles got to the ground and stood ready to assist Marcus, should the crutch fail him. A second carriage was visible in the predawn light, and beside it stood the baron and two other men. The three turned as Marcus alit from the carriage.

"Present him with the weapons," Marcus told Charles. "The choice of pistols can be made at any time. But I would see the paper concerning the wager before he accepts a weapon."

With a nod, Charles removed the pistol case from the carriage and crossed to where the baron stood. While he conversed with the three, a brace of carriages carrying the earl and the elder Rothschild sons arrived. Seconds behind those carriages came four more bearing persons who had been present at the gala the previous evening. From one of these stepped the old viscount. He glanced around the area and, locating Marcus, moved to greet him.

"This is a day for such a thing," he said coming up to Marcus, "if indeed there is such a day at all."

"Any day will suffice, my friend," Marcus answered.

"The word of your return and the challenge has spread over the countryside like wildfire, Marcus. 'Tis enough to bring the loftiest of men from his chambers early."

"Aye, you're correct, I suppose. Men will ever take pleasure in the chance of another's death."

"Ah, Marcus," the earl said, drawing near. "How goes the morning, sir?"

"As well as one could expect when such things are afoot, my lord," Marcus answered. "Even now Charles returns with the document of the wager." Slipping a hand inside his waistcoat, he removed a folded document, and when Charles presented the baron's to him, said, "I think he will find all in order, Charles. Have you perused this contract?"

"I have, Marcus. It would seem the one gentleman with the baron is his solicitor, the other, his second. His solicitor assures me that the document is complete."

"Then I shall scan it closely," Marcus smiled. "Would that there could be an end to the ways of conniving solicitors so that honest men could remain so." He accepted the document and allowed Charles to take the one he had prepared. Then, in silence, he studied the conditions of the wager and with a nod handed the contract to the earl. "Does it consider all it should, Lord Rothschild?"

The earl read the document thoroughly before handing it back to Marcus with a nod. "It is complete, Marcus. An accounting of my idiocy. You may yet recall your words, Marcus. It seems over much you bear on your shoulders for the Rothschilds."

Ignoring the statement, Marcus said, "It seems the baron is prepared. He even now makes his choice of pistols." Seconds later Charles turned from the baron and returned to Marcus, the paper of the wager in one hand, the pistol chest in the other.

"The baron wishes that a party other than a Rothschild retain the documents. It would seem he does not trust our family."

The viscount stepped forward and extended a hand. "It would be my pleasure to do it, Charles."

When the two contracts had been tendered to the old man, Marcus and the baron moved to position on the dueling site.

"A fine morning for an Englishman to die," the baron said as he turned his back to Marcus.

"Or to kill," Marcus amended, letting the crutch fall from under his arm.

Charles and the baron's second took their places to observe that the rules of sportsmanship were met. Upon a nod from the Prussian's man, Charles said, "Begin the pace when I speak the command. Upon your tenth step, you will turn and fire. Understood by both parties?"

"Understood," the baron growled. "You are but ten steps from death, Englishman."

"Get on with it," Marcus said.

"Very well," Charles said. "Pace." He then called the paces off to the count of ten.

On the final count, both combatants turned. The pistols came to bear. Silence held the small park in its grip for half a breath, then smoke blossomed from the Prussian's weapon.

Hard on the heels of the discharge which interrupted the morning stillness, Marcus jerked as if in spasm, nearly losing the balance of his injured ankle. A furrow of blood cascading over the whiteness of bone appeared along the left side of his head above the ear. He shook himself and raised a hand to the bleeding groove. His fingers were tinged bright with blood when he brought his hand away to glance at it. Then he again brought the pistol to bear, his movements measured and sure.

"Well, Baron," he said as the pistol leveled and

became steady, "it would seem the Prussians have this day reached the point of ill luck."

The Prussian had paled when Marcus failed to fall. At the words, his eyes widened and his mouth opened. The sharp intake of his breath could be heard throughout the glen. Fear crept into his eyes and manner.

Marcus laughed shortly, saying, "I have no desire to kill you, Prussian. Would you agree that the match and the wager are mine?"

Disbelief flooded over the baron's features. His glance went from Marcus to the seconds and then to the watching crowd.

"Make haste with your decision, Baron," Marcus said. "I do hunger."

The Prussian eyes swung back to center on Marcus. Suddenly the flush of embarrassment swept the paleness from his features. "Bah!" he snarled, throwing the pistol from him.

"Hold, Prussian," Marcus called. "Your word that the day is mine, or your life. The choice is yours, but take not another step until that choice is voiced."

The command caught the man in mid-stride. He halted. His chest expanded with the heavy breath he inhaled. "This day is yours, Englishman. Enjoy it."

"I shall," Marcus answered, allowing the flint of his pistol to ease down. Then Charles, the earl and the elder Rothschild heirs were at him.

"Aye, Marcus, fantastic," Charles said. "But what of your wound?"

Marcus stood silently until the Prussian carriage had gone from the glen. Then, with a glance at Charles, he raised a hand to his wound and, in the same moment, collapsed in a heap at their feet.

"Quickly!" the earl exclaimed. "To the carriage with him." He turned on his eldest sons. "Move! Assist the man who gave you your futures. Move, I say."

Robroy and Montgomery moved under the lashing tongue of their father. Hastily they lifted Marcus and moved him to the seat of the carriage. Then, before they had the door shut, Charles was at the lines screaming commands to the steeds.

Penelope sat staring at the food before her, an expression of impending doom on her features. Beside her, a concerned Becky said, "My lady, you concern yourself for naught. The duke will be fine. So have some food lest you sicken."

Penelope shook her head and pointed toward the window. "Even now the sun has risen, Becky. Ah, my very life might at this moment be lying—dead." Suddenly she pushed the plate back and placed her head on folded arms. "I fear for him, Becky. He must not die. God, allow him to kill the baron."

"Aye and I would wager that has been done, my lady," the maid answered. "Dry your eyes. God would not allow such as he to perish."

Penelope's head came up. "Listen," she said, silencing the maid. "I hear a carriage traveling at outrageous speed." Pushing back from the table, she ran from the room to the steps of Rothschild Halls.

Charles swung the carriage into the drive at full tilt and brought it to a stop at the steps. Instantly he was off the seat and opening the door. "Hurry, Pen," he called, the urgency in his voice making the words a command. "Call the servants. Marcus is hurt."

The news was enough to tear her heart from her breast. Stifling a sob, she turned and ran back into the halls, calling for the servants as she went.

At the carriage, Charles studied his friend and said, "Ah, Marcus, you do give so much of yourself. Know that the Rothschilds will do everything possible for you."

The eyelids moved slightly. The orbs of blue—dimmed to a slate gray—barely shone. The corner of the mouth twitched into the beginning of a smile. "Charles?" Marcus moaned.

"Here, Marcus," Charles answered, bending closer. "The servants come even now. Hold, friend." He moved to allow the servants to lift the injured man. "Let not your clumsy hands jostle him," he ordered as they brought Marcus from the carriage.

Penelope stood with fist to mouth, her teeth set on a finger to hold back the sobs. She turned as the men carried their burden up the steps. "Come," she ordered, leading the way. "I shall prepare his bed." Then she was up the stairs as fast as her flying feet would carry her. "Hot water, Becky. And ointment," she called as she ran.

Charles waited no longer. Turning, he bounded to the carriage seat and once again screamed at the steeds, sending them away from the halls toward the town and medical help.

Penelope stood encircled by the earl's arm, watching the ministrations of the surgeon. A sob shook her and the arm around her shoulders tightened.

"Have faith, lass," her father told her. "The man who lies in that bed will not allow the angel of death to have his way."

"He cannot die, Father. He cannot."

The doctor turned from the bed and faced them. "What can be done has been," he said. "The ball touched naught that is vital. Though what has occurred within the skull from such a blow is not known."

"Will he die?" Charles asked.

"No," was the answer, "I would guess not. The ball bared the bone of the skull, but other than that there is little damage. I shall call on the morrow and see to him."

"Thank God," Penelope breathed at his words. "Thank God, he will live."

CHAPTER ELEVEN

Butter-yellow candlelight forced its way between his lids and a moan of pain escaped from his lips. Motion from the bedside was immediate, and a body moved to place itself between him and the light.

He heard a voice filled with misery murmur softly, "Oh, Marcus, would that I could draw the pain from you and into my own body." Then the engulfing blackness of unconsciousness swept all else from him and he slept.

Daylight filled the chamber when he again became conscious. For a moment, he lay with eyes closed, aware of the sounds of other people around him. Then, opening his eyes, he beheld a wrinkled, leather-skinned face peering at him. Behind that unfamiliar face stood Penelope, Charles and the earl.

"Remain still," the wrinkled one ordered. "I would inspect your wound." Fingers touched his skull, bringing instant pain with them.

"You must be the agent of the baron," Marcus said as the pain grew more intense with every movement of the fingers. "Do you intend to finish what the Prussian began?"

"The pistol's ball was within a hair of doing for you, Marcus. Would that you had killed him for his efforts," Charles told him.

"What day is this?" Marcus asked.

"It was yesterday that you returned the fortunes of the Rothschilds, Marcus. Worry not of the day, for it will be many before you are about again. Rest and allow the Rothschilds to express their gratitude."

"He has little choice in the matter," the doctor announced. "He'll not retain balance should he leave this bed."

Penelope stepped forward as the doctor moved from the bedside. "Marcus, would that I be allowed to minister to you. It would please me."

A smile pulled his lips. " 'Tis a child you would make of me, Penny, a child to be nursed from the vapors. This wound of mine is naught but a nuisance."

"A nuisance which could have cost your life," the earl said, moving to stand beside his daughter. "We are—all the Rothschilds—in your debt for evermore, my lord."

" 'Tis naught you owe me, my lord," Marcus replied. " 'Twas a pleasure watching the Prussian's displeasure at having his life spared."

"Marcus," Penelope asked again, "may I be allowed to care for you until you regain your health?"

He hesitated, an expression of deep thought on his face. " 'Twould be amiss if I refused my hostess her wish," he said finally, a smile taking him.

"Hah!" Charles exploded. "It seems the baby Rothschild was concerned for a moment there."

Penelope did not try to hide her embarrassment. Turning to her brother, she asked, "And is it above your station to wish to assist he who has performed such marvels for the Rothschild family, Charles?"

Caught unawares by the statement, Charles stood

still for a moment before saying, "Oh, sister, I think you intentionally misunderstood my intent. I—"

"Enough," the earl demanded. "Enough of this childishness." He turned to the doctor. "What of his food and drink, sir?"

The doctor shrugged. "Whatever be his pleasure, my lord. There's nothing that can increase his pain. I shall return two days hence and see to him." He sent a glance at Penelope. "Continue use of the ointment and see that he does not tire himself."

"I shall," she answered happily. "I shall be observant of his every move."

"Very well, then," the doctor answered with a smile. "But he may suffer more from overattendance than from the wound. I shall visit in two days."

When the doctor had gone, the earl sent a glance at Marcus and said, "My lord, the two eldest sons of the Rothschilds would attend you to pay their respects and express their gratitude."

A grimace of displeasure came to the wounded man's face. "I would have them save their gratitude and their respects for one who wishes them," he answered. "I did nothing intentionally to aid them. My thoughts were for the three of you only."

The earl bowed. "As you will, my lord. They shall be so informed." He turned to leave the room.

"My lord Earl," Marcus called, "please refrain from using my title when you speak to me. Though it is true I have again accepted the cloak of dukedom, I prefer my friends to know me as Marcus."

"Habit is a terrible master, Marcus," the earl answered. "And it is many years of habit I must master to refrain from use of the title at times. I shall try." Then he was out of the room, leaving Penelope and Charles behind.

"You have breathed new life into my father, Marcus," Penelope said. "It's been a long while since I've seen him so happy."

"And," Charles added, "he has taken an oath never to confront the gaming tables again. It will dull his spirit of wager, but it has been an enlightening time for him, Marcus."

"For us all," Marcus answered. "Let us pray that all have learned from the experience."

"The baron has, I'll wager," Charles answered. "Though what he has learned is beyond telling."

Penelope suddenly gasped. "Marcus, it has been well over a day since you have eaten. Are you not hungry?"

"Ravenous. And thirsty, too. Would there be wine?"

"Of course. I shall not be long," she called over her shoulder as she ran from the room.

"Ah, Marcus," Charles asked when she'd gone from earshot, "what now, my friend?"

"I don't know, Charles. The burden of dukedom rests heavily on my mind. Whether to again abandon it and return to America or to remain in England and abide the ways of court is a question which preys."

"And what of my sister?"

Marcus was silent for a long moment. Finally he nodded. "Would that she was of an age to know her mind, Charles. But she is yet a child. Should her emotions be so guided at a later date, it will be time enough to broach such a subject."

"But you do care for her, Marcus. You have stated such to me. And there can be little question in either of our minds that she cares for you."

"Possibly. But first loves are not as intense as many have thought. Within the passing of seven days, she will find the ardor cooled, if I guess correctly."

"I think you err in that respect, Marcus. 'Tis an ardor which would not cool in as many years, I'll wager."

"We shall see, Charles. We shall see."

The sounds of the girl's returning silenced them on the subject, and she burst into the chambers with wine vessel in hand. "Becky will arrive shortly with food, Marcus," she announced. "I thought your thirst should be quenched first, though."

Accepting the drink, he smiled his thanks and tipped the mug to his lips. When he'd lowered it, he sighed heavily. "Ah, 'tis welcome the wine is. My thanks, Penny, but I fear you shall regret your position of nurse before long."

"Never, Marcus. Do you think of me as a child who flits from one interest to another without care for any?"

Charles laughed. "An apt description, sister. Well, there is much to be done. I'll leave and not bother you, Marcus. Should you have need of anything, just let me know."

On the fourth day following the duel, Marcus awoke to find Penelope asleep in a chair beside the bed. For several minutes, he lay silently, watching the innocence of the girl in the unguarded moment. Then, with cautious movements, he removed the coverlet and quietly got to his feet. There was an instant when he clung to the footpost of the bed as wave after wave of nausea swept over him, but finally his head ceased its swimming and he straightened.

His initial step was a cautious one. The nightshirt he wore threatened to trip him up if he but erred in a single movement. Then, one step after the other, he made his way to the door of the chamber, stopped a moment to rest, then returned to his bed. A smile of satisfaction was on his lips when he again settled under the cover and glanced at the still-sleeping girl.

Moments later his eyes were still on her when she whimpered softly and twisted slightly. Her eyelids fluttered momentarily, then opened completely. Instantly she turned to view her patient.

"Ah, Marcus," she exclaimed, stifling a yawn, "it seems I did sleep."

"And much needed it was," he answered. "There is no need for you to spend every waking hour at my side, lass. Any danger there was is past."

She got to her feet with a grimace of pain from the ungainly position in the chair. "Till the day you are again on your feet, Marcus, I shall attend you. The Rothschilds do not allow their saviors to fall in need of anything."

He chuckled softly at the statement. "Do the Rothschilds also desire their youngest child to become old before her time? The night in the chair has done you ill, lass. Go freshen yourself lest your bones knit in the position of that infernal seat."

She nodded. "I think you're correct, Marcus. 'Tis a witch I must resemble. I shall see to my toilet and return with our morning meal."

When she had gone from the room, he again slipped from the bed and stood a moment in anticipation of a dizzy spell. When none came, he moved across the room and retrieved his clothing. Several minutes later, he was attired and sitting upright on the edge of the bed. He was like that when Charles knocked on the chamber door and entered.

"Ho, Marcus, and what are you about? Is there no injury you respect?" the younger man demanded on seeing his friend.

"I'm tired of this bed, comfortable though it may be," Marcus answered. "I would begin the process of healing in a standing position."

"But my sister will be much ired at your leaving the bed so soon, Marcus. 'Tis on your head the anger will fall." He cast a glance around the room and asked, "And where is the crutch, Marcus? Did you manage all this without the stick of wood?"

Marcus nodded. "Aye, and quite well. It would seem the extended time within the confines of the bed has seen to the sprain. There is but a slight twitch of pain at times."

"And the head wound?"

Marcus raised a hand to touch the bandage at his head. He smiled shortly. "The pain has lessened to the point of an ache. I believe I shall survive. But what of the family, Charles? Are the Rothschilds all in good health?"

"We are all excellent, Marcus. Several of those who attended the party have sent notes of congratulations and concern. The viscount requests audience at the earliest possible moment your condition will allow."

Penelope stepped into the room at that moment. She halted on the threshold, her eyes going wide as they fell on the fully dressed Marcus. "Marcus," she got out, "you are about!" Then her glance filled with anger and she turned to her brother. "Charles, are you mad? What are you thinking of to take him from his bed at such an early date? Have you no sense at all in you?"

"Hold, lass," Marcus called. " 'Twas none of your brother's doing. I was as I am now when he entered, so you needn't lash him for that which is not his doing."

She sent a suspicious glance at him and again looked at her brother. " 'Tis a good thing, my brother, that Marcus takes your side, else I should have your head." She turned to Marcus. "Marcus, you still should not be about. The wound is—"

"Better," he interrupted. "Lord, lass, do you expect me to remain on my backside for the extent of my life?"

"But your ankle . . ."

"The ankle is all better. Now, if the two of you will be of assistance to me, I should like to leave this room for a short time. I would attempt the stairs if I could but have you accompany me."

Instantly the two Rothschilds moved to his side.

"Not lift me, accompany me," he protested. He pushed himself to his feet and, for a moment, stood quietly. "As you see, I am capable of stance. Let us see if I am also capable of motion for a period of time."

"There is no need, Marcus," Penelope pleaded. "Allow the wound more time to mend. It would do little for any of us if you were to plummet down the stairs."

He chuckled at her concern. "I shall endeavor not to plummet, then, Penny. Come, accompany me." He stepped away from the bed with caution riding his steps.

"He will as always, Pen," Charles said, "so we should accompany him under his terms, lest he attempt the stairs by himself."

Several long minutes later they stood at the foot of the stairs. Marcus breathed heavily at the exertion. "I think the ball did sap the strength from my body," he said with a smile at Penelope.

"And the brains from your head," she answered, her smile belying the weight of the words. "You should still be resting, Marcus. This is nonsense."

"But necessary for one such as I, Penny. Charles will tell you that I sicken if I remain abed too long."

"But Charles would swear oath to whatever you state, Marcus," she answered. " 'Tis the both of you I shall be wary of."

He laughed at the accusation, saying, "I would spend a moment of rest on the terrace if the weather allows. It is fresh air my lungs are needing."

"Then we shall breakfast there," she answered. "If your balance is such, I will take my leave and see to the meal."

"Go, Pen," Charles ordered. "I shall tend him. He'll not fall."

When she'd gone from them, Charles studied his friend a moment before asking, "Is your wind returned to normal, Marcus? It would seem you gasp less."

"Aye, Charles. My lungs do fill easier. Let us make our way out to the table."

Standing ready to assist should the need arise, Charles paced beside his friend until the terrace had been reached. When Marcus had sunk into a chair, the youngest Rothschild son asked, "Something concerns you, my friend?"

Marcus nodded. "Aye, friend Charles. I cannot seem to get the dukedom out of my mind now. Would that I could return to the rank of commoner and have done with this."

Charles smiled at his friend's words. " 'Tis passing strange," he muttered. "What most would happily give their all for, you would have none of. Though the manners of the court bore me, I feel England, for all her ways, is where I shall remain."

Marcus nodded. "The several days past have shown your love for the mother country. I sensed it earlier."

"And what of yourself, Marcus? Have you yet decided whether it shall be mother England or America for you?"

Marcus shook his head. "No. There are influences from both which draw strongly at me. My interests in America require attention, as do those of the dukedom. I am torn."

"Ah, and is it love for England which pulls against America—or love of something more human, my friend?"

"You will persevere, Charles. It has been my thought, though, that should I return to America and conclude my interests there, and should your sister be on my return as you believe her to be now, I would speak with your father of her."

"You're wasting precious time, my friend. Pen would have you this instant. And there's no one in this household who would be anything but happy about it."

Their conversation was brought to an end by the appearance of the earl. "Fair morning, Marcus and Charles," he greeted as he stepped to the table and seated himself. He sent a concerned look at Marcus, asking, "Do you not endanger the wound with such early movement, Marcus?"

"As I've told Charles, the pain has subsided to naught but an ache," Marcus answered. "I think the exercise will speed the healing."

"Marcus concerns himself with his reacquired station, Father," Charles informed the earl. "Would that all should have no more concern than such."

For a long moment, the earl let his glance go to the grounds of the Rothschild estate. Then, with a nod, he said, "Aye, Charles, and you too shall know the concern he bears when it is your responsibility to mind such a position. There is much that lies unseen to those who view from the outside."

"Ah, well," Marcus said, "what will come will come. There is naught I shall be able to do about it this day." He turned his attention to Charles, "I would have a messenger sent to my solicitors, as there is much to be done concerning the dukedom. Many things must be brought up to date."

"As soon as the meal is finished, Marcus," Charles assured him as Penelope stepped to the terrace. "Ah, sister dear, is it that we are to starve in our own home?"

She seated herself before saying, "Patience, Charles. Even now the food is coming. I think you will survive until it is arrived."

"There are many who send their respects, Marcus," the earl said, ignoring his children and their humorous bantering. "And no end to galas which are planned in your honor."

"There is much I must do, Lord Rothschild. I shall have little time for such recreation at the present."

Penelope chuckled at his statement. "Must you be so sober, Marcus? I am certain the dukedom will survive if all is not done in one day."

" 'Tis his return to America which concerns him, sister," Charles said as a manservant and a maid stepped onto the terrace with the morning meal.

Penelope sat for a moment, her stricken glance on her brother. Then, with catching breath, she stood, saying, "I fear my hunger has fled, Father. I would be excused."

The earl studied her for a moment, then asked, "Are you ill, child?"

"No, Father. 'Tis nothing. I would return to my bed and rest a moment."

Marcus's eyes were on her as she swung from the table and left the terrace. "Penny spent too long tending me rather than seeing to her own health," he said, genuine concern in his tone.

"Youth will out," the earl answered. "Don't concern yourself, Marcus. She will recover, but I fear it is not the lack of rest which affects her."

"Then what, my lord?"

Rothschild sent a meaningful look at Charles. "I feel Charles should be told of the request you made of me on the day of the gala, Marcus. For it is his words which have sent my daughter to her bed."

"What do you mean, Father?" Charles asked, leaning forward and looking from the earl to Marcus. "Is there some secret of which I should be aware?"

"Charles is aware of the affection I hold for Penny, my lord," Marcus said. "Though I am certain it was not intentional. I believe he—"

"Oh, by all that's holy!" Charles interrupted. "My mention of Marcus returning to America! I am a complete fool. Of course, Father, you are correct. I shall go speak with her."

"Hold," the earl ordered. "Is it true that the duke is to return to America?"

Marcus nodded. "I must, my lord. I have many interests there which require my attendance and attention."

"Then, Charles, don't go to your sister." He turned to Marcus. "Is it your intention to leave without informing her of your feelings, Marcus? For if it is, I must inform you that she has confessed her love for you to me. I would not have my daughter injured if it is within my power to prevent it."

"She is but a child," Marcus said. "If she were of the experience to know . . ."

"That is not a reason, Marcus," Charles said. "While it's true Pen has had little concern for those who have sought her attentions, it's not as if she has had no chance of learning of emotions. I believe you are the first she has met whom she deems truly a man. I, like Father, believe she should be made aware of your feelings for her before you leave."

A manservant stepped to the terrace at that moment to announce the arrival of the viscount.

Grimacing at the interruption, the earl said in a lowered voice, "Marcus, consider this question thoroughly, for both yourself and Penelope."

"Ah, my lord Rothschild," the aging viscount said, coming to the terrace, "I regret interrupting your meal, but there is news I would share with all of you."

"The meal is of little importance," the earl said, "since we have not as yet touched a morsel. Seat yourself and inform us of this news."

With a word of greeting to Charles and Marcus, the old man sank into the chair vacated earlier by Penelope. " 'Tis word of your dueling foe I carry this morning, Marcus."

"The baron?" Rothschild asked. "What is it he has devised for evil now?"

"Nay, not for evil," the viscount answered, "but for the good of England, I think. He has arranged for passage to the continent and he returns to his native

Prussia. 'Tis a great favor you have performed for all England, Marcus. 'Tis because of you he goes. Your act of allowing him to live has brought the expression of scorn upon him from all who are aware of what has passed. It is this which drives him from our shores."

Charles sighed. "For myself, whatever his reason, I am glad that he is going. England has no need for such as he."

"True," the earl agreed, "but I am amiss. Let us all eat. Join us, my lord Viscount."

"No," the old man declined. " 'Twas early this morning when I broke my fast. I go now to share the news with those others who would see the last of the Prussian." He got unsteadily to his feet and, with a final word to the three of them, left.

When the old man had entered the house, the earl returned his attention to Marcus. "Of the matter of Penelope, Marcus. Consider closely your actions, lest both of you lose. Now that shall be the extent of my interference in the matter. Let us eat. The food, I am certain, will be as good as the viscount's news."

"Is something still troubling you, Marcus?" Charles asked, his eyes on his friend.

"The news of the baron's leaving. The man didn't appear as one who would concern himself with the scorn of others. Doesn't it seem odd he allows such a thing to drive him from these shores?"

"His pride was dealt a fierce blow by your actions, Marcus," Rothschild said. "Do you think he would ignore the slights of those who earlier respected him?"

"I suppose I imagine ghosts where there are none. That he is going is reason enough for elation."

"Well said," Charles agreed. "And it is correct you are, Father; the food is delicious."

When they had finished the meal, Marcus got to his feet, saying, "I would spend time in self-counsel, my friends. The matter of Penelope is indeed one which must be seen to. I shall exercise my body and my thoughts for a while." With that, he stepped from the terrace to the grounds of the estate.

"Take care the head wound does not do you in, Marcus," Charles called after him.

Upon taking her leave from the table, Penelope ran up the stairs to her chambers and threw herself across the bed. Her sobs were muffled only slightly by the coverlet as she wept out her frustrations. Just moments after she'd entered the chambers, Becky entered and set about consoling her mistress.

"Come, come, my lady," she pleaded. "What upsets you so?"

After several heavy sobs, Penelope rolled to her back, saying, "Oh, Becky, he is returning to America. I shan't ever see him again."

" 'Tis the duke you speak of, my lady?"

Penelope nodded. "He goes back across the sea, away from me. Ah, Becky, am I so ugly that he has noticed me not?"

"He has noticed you, my lady," the maid assured her. " 'Twas my thought that he had been taken with you. Come, dry your eyes, my lady. He is but a man and, as such does not know his own mind. But take heart. He has not yet gone from these shores."

Gaining control of her sobbing, Penelope dried her eyes with the back of her hand. "But he makes plans to do so, even now. There is naught I can consider to force him to stay. Ah, what shall I do?"

"Maybe you need a breath of the fresh air, my lady," Becky advised. "You will feel better if you will but go for a walk."

Penelope sat in thought for a long moment before saying, "Aye, and it cannot hurt. It is a ride I shall be taking, Becky. Will you see to the preparation of my mount?"

Becky nodded reluctantly. "Yes, my lady. I would

accompany you if I might, lest the steed give trouble you do not expect."

A smile of understanding tugged at Penelope's lips. "My Becky. You do worry about me at all times. Very well, we shall both ride. Perhaps a good ride will jar my thoughts and bring to mind a method by which I may keep the duke on English soil."

"I shall have the horses readied, my lady," Becky said in relief as she turned to leave the room.

Marcus was resting in a bower, his thoughts on the problem of his heart's desire, when the sound of hoofbeats caught his attention. He glanced up in time to glimpse the steeds bearing Penelope and the maid as they made their way down the path toward the elder Rothschild son's estate. The sight of the girl set his nerves tingling and he stood, hoping to catch their attention and to speak with her. The two rode on, and after a moment, he muttered, "Time enough to tell her of my decision upon her return." Turning back to Rothschild Halls, he searched out the earl and, finding him in the library, announced, "I would speak with you and your son, my lord."

The earl eyed him for a heartbeat before calling to a manservant and sending for Charles. "Is it of Penelope you would speak, Marcus?" he asked when the servant had gone.

Marcus nodded. "It is, my lord. I have come to a decision which I would discuss with you and Charles."

Rothschild could read nothing in the other man's expression. "Would you have some wine, Marcus? The morning is warm and you perspire."

" 'Tis not the temperature which has its way with me," Marcus answered. "Ah, here's Charles."

"What?" Charles asked as he entered the library. "Is your wound worsened, Marcus?"

"Not my wound, Charles. I would speak of Penelope to both you and your father, if I may."

Charles glanced from his friend to his father, saying, "You have come to a decision on the matter, then?"

"I have," Marcus answered. "My Lord Rothschild, please permit me to speak of marriage to Penny. It would be an empty world without her, and though—"

"'Tis a miracle," Charles interrupted, "that I should, indeed, have you as a brother. Father, what do you think? Is this not the finest of days for the family Rothschild?"

The earl sat looking at Marcus. Tears formed in the old man's eyes and he nodded. "Aye, my son, 'tis that. Ah, Marcus, you need not ask. My feelings toward you are well known. Go to her now, for the disclosure of such a thing will fill her with happiness."

Relief and embarrassment were obvious on Marcus's face. Then Charles was gripping his hand and slapping his back in congratulations.

"Ah, Marcus," the happy young man exclaimed, "you do gladden the hearts of the Rothschilds. But go, my friend. Tell Pen what she has ached to hear since first laying eyes upon you. Go."

"She is at this moment riding with her abigail. On her return, I shall speak my troth to her. Lord willing, she will accept."

The earl laughed heartily at the prayer. "Charles, it seems your friend, though wise in worldly matters, knows little of the ways of women. Accept, my dear Marcus? The girl will, lest I mistake her, be overcome with joy."

"Then, Marcus," Charles asked, "have you decided to remain in England?"

Marcus nodded. "Aye. 'Twill be necessary for me to return to America to see to my holdings there. I had thought Penny, if she is agreeable to my offer, would accompany me on the voyage. She had expressed a desire to familiarize herself with the country."

"By all that's holy," Charles exclaimed, "though it is yet morning, I shall require wine to properly celebrate this occurrence. Join me, Father? Marcus?"

The earl moved to offer his hand to Marcus. "Though you detest the use of such things, I feel I must." He bowed over the hand of the younger man, saying, "My lord Duke, you have favored the Rothschilds beyond all that could be imagined on this day."

A grimace took Marcus's lips, then turned into a smile. " 'Tis wine we need, as Charles suggests, my lord."

Charles was already filling vessels. When the chore was completed, he lifted two of the drinks and handed them to Marcus and the earl. Taking the final one for himself, he lifted it in toast. "To our new family member, Father."

"Aye, and to the honor he bestows on the Rothschilds this day," the earl answered, lifting his drink in kind.

"To the fairest of the kingdom and my heart's desire," Marcus said.

CHAPTER TWELVE

" 'Tis a fine day, m'lady," Becky said after many minutes of riding silently. "Are you not feeling better?"

Penelope sat the steed as if she had not heard. Her back was rigid.

"M'lady?" the abigail persisted.

Finally Penelope turned to fix the maid with a vacant glance. "I would rest at yonder tree, Becky," she said, pulling the reins to slow the mount.

When they had dismounted, Becky asked, "Is it your brothers we go to see, m'lady? Will you ask advice from them?"

"Hah!" Penelope snorted. "Ask those who would at this moment, had it not been for Marcus, have me married to that oaf of a Prussian? 'Tis only chance which has brought me in this direction. Nay, I shall not visit my brothers on this day or any other."

The abigail nodded in understanding. " 'Twas a vile thing they suggested in consideration of their own interests, m'lady. Have you a thought of method for keeping the duke on English soil?"

Penelope shook her head. "No. Would that it were proper for me to go to him with words of my love for him. Would that I might express my feelings to him."

"Oh," Becky sighed, " 'twould be the upsetting of all who heard of such a thing. And of such note if he did . . ."

"If he found humor in the words I uttered?" Penelope asked. "Aye, and well he might. For to him, I am a child. One who knows nothing of her feelings. 'Tis a . . ." She broke off, listening for sound in the clear air of the day. "Is it a carriage I hear, Becky?"

The abigail listened intently for a moment before nodding. " 'Tis that, m'lady. And coming fast."

"Ah, that it could be Marcus at the reins of such flying steeds," Penelope muttered. "That it could be he, coming for me in fear that he might lose my love—"

A carriage topped a hill from the direction in which they had come. At the sight of it, Becky said, "Alas, m'lady, 'tis the black carriage which was earlier noticed to the east of Rothschild Halls. There was the mending of a wheel to be seen to, I was told by the servant who was sent to ask if the Rothschilds could offer assistance."

The maid's tone brought a sad smile to the face of Penelope. "Ah, Becky, I did not truly believe the carriage would have Marcus at the lines. 'Tis a dreamer I am." Her glance went back to the approaching carriage.

" 'Twould appear the driver of that carriage has concern for others," Becky said. "Even now, he slows to prevent our being dusted by the wheels."

The black carriage with its equally black steeds had slowed by half by the time the women could make out the driver's features. Then, when it was nearly alongside their position, the driver called a command to the horses and drew the carriage to a stop.

"Ah, good day, ladies," the pockmarked man said,

doffing his hat to Penelope and the maid. "Out for a relaxing ride, is it?"

Penelope nodded. " 'Tis our thanks you have for not dusting us, sir," she answered, turning to mount her horse.

"Hold, lady," he called as the carriage door opened. " 'Tis a word we would have with you this fine day."

Penelope turned back to face the driver and discovered three ruffian-appearing men stepping from the coach. Her glance went to Becky. In tremulous voice, she said, "We would complete our ride, sir. Come, Becky."

"No. Not this day," the leader of those from the carriage said, reaching to clutch her arm. " 'Tis a carriage ride you'll take now, lass."

Anger coupled with fear flooded over Penelope at the man's iron grip and growling words. She attempted to pull free of his clutches as Becky advanced to strike at him.

"Release her," Becky ordered fiercely as she beat upon the man's head and shoulders. "Release my mistress lest I—"

Her statement was cut short by the coarse bag which was pulled over her head.

Penelope, her glance going to the third man who had stepped from the interior of the carriage, took note of the similar bag he carried and, with a frantic jerk, freed her arm from the man who held her. She turned to run and had taken but two steps when she was again caught and a blinding, dust-filled bag was drawn over her head and shoulders.

"They are not to be injured. 'Twas his order," she heard the driver's voice say as she was suddenly enclosed in a bearlike grip and lifted from her feet. "Take care in your method of handling them."

Her attempt at screaming brought her nothing but a mouthful of heavy dust. She choked and, due to the clamp of arms around her, could not regain her breath for a long moment. Her eyes burned from the dust, bringing tears and frustration, and she kicked violently at the ruffian who held her. Then, without warning, she was thrown to the floor of the carriage atop a kicking, mumbling Becky. The maid's movements ceased as her mistress's weight settled against her. In the next moment, the sound of the carriage door was heard and the horses were again called to. Then the rocking of the carriage told them they were in motion at high speed through the countryside.

Only moments later, a voice said, "Bind their wrists. I think we'll have a fight should they be allowed to regain their feet."

Rough hands clutched Penelope's wrists, and a string was pulled tight around them. The action brought a renewal of her kicking movements, but to no avail. A pair of hands settled on her ankles and held them solidly. She rode, face down in the carriage, the bag blinding her, to a destination unknown.

"Aye, ladies," a male voice said, "that's the way. Just you relax and enjoy the ride. 'Twill not be long before you can remove the bags from your heads." The words were followed by a harsh laugh.

"'Tis a good piece of work we've done," another voice said. "His lordship will be pleased."

"Aye, two for the same as one," the third voice added. "'Tis a bargain he's getting with this day's efforts."

Penelope was aware of the words but unconscious of their meaning as the carriage swept along the rough surface of the road.

After what seemed an eternity, the carriage slowed and drew to a stop. The two women were taken from the carriage, the bags still covering them, and led into a stone-floored chamber. Penelope, her anger and discomfort overwhelming her, mumbled oaths at the men who handled her. Her protestations were answered by a coarse laugh; then the bonds at her wrists were removed and she felt the tingling ache of new blood flowing into her fingertips.

"You can remove the bags yourselves, ladies," one of the three abductors said. Then the sound of a door being closed and bolted came to them.

Hastily, every move of her fingers bringing pain, Penelope pulled the filthy bag from her upper body and threw it aside. A mumbling string of oaths brought her about and she reached to assist the abigail in removing the bag which confined her.

"Ah, m'lady," Becky exclaimed, breathing deeply. "What has become of us?"

Penelope wiped at the dust left by the bag and sent a glance around the chamber where they were held captive. "I know only as much as do you, Becky," she said after a moment. "We have been kidnapped, but for what reason and designed by whom, I know not."

"Oh, m'lady, 'tis fear for our lives I have within my bosom. What vile—"

"No, Becky," Penelope said, in voice more brave than she felt. "Had it been our lives they wished, we would not have been placed in this chamber, and we'd have been dead by now. No, try not the door, for I heard the bolt shot home when our abductors departed." She again sent her glance around the room and moved toward a window.

Moving the drapes aside, she said, "Alas, we'll gain naught here, for the portal is boarded over."

"M'lady, I do fear that we . . ." Becky began, tears streaming down her face.

"Enough of that, Becky," Penelope ordered sternly. "I know not what awaits us. 'Tis my thought that before long, my family and Marcus will discover us missing. They will, I wager, demand just payment for the acts which have been performed against us this day. Now, dry your eyes and let us study on what we can do to remove ourselves from this place."

* * *

It was nearing mid-day when Charles entered the library and asked the earl if his sister had returned.

"No. 'Tis upset she was," the earl answered the query. "She is probably holding counsel with herself over this matter of Marcus leaving. Still, she has been absent a long time." He got from his chair. "And where is Marcus, Charles?"

"I have this moment completed the chore of replacing the bandage on his head. It is by his wish that I came to seek Penelope."

Marcus stepped into the room at that moment. His glance swept swiftly around the room and his eyes thinned to slits. "What?" he asked. "No sign yet of Penny's return?"

"None, Marcus," Charles answered.

"We concern ourselves for naught," the earl said. "Her abigail was accompanying her. There is naught could occur of which we would not be informed." He turned as Robroy swept into the room. "What is it, Rob?" he asked. "I see anger in your eyes."

Robroy's glance met Marcus's and he bowed stiffly from the waist. "My lord Duke, I shan't impress my company on you over long." He looked at his father and said, "Is someone of this house without sense or care concerning horseflesh, Father?"

"What is this nonsense you growl at me?" the earl demanded.

"I chose to ride on the road in this direction rather than across the estates. And what appears but a mile from here but two of the steeds from your own stables. They are tied to a bush and abandoned. From the saddles, I guessed my sister had left them to their own devices. Has she no respect for animals of such breeding, Father?"

At the words, both Charles and Marcus moved forward. Marcus reached to clutch the man's arm, saying,

"Enough of your petty ways. Make haste. Where were the horses located when you came upon them?"

Robroy faced Marcus, attempting to pull away from him. "My lord Duke, I think you do me an injustice. Release me."

"You blithering dandy," Charles snapped, "answer him. Where did you locate the horses?"

"Father, I . . ." the eldest Rothschild son protested.

"Come," the earl ordered. "You shall show us." He called to a manservant and ordered the saddling of three horses.

Releasing his grip on Robroy's arm, Marcus turned and made his way from the house. When he stood on the porch, he cast a glance along the road in the direction he'd last seen Penelope and the abigail riding. Charles came up behind him and also searched the vacant road.

"What do you think, Marcus?" he asked after a period of time.

" 'Tis with dread I consider what passes through my mind, Charles," Marcus answered. "It can only be abduction. 'Tis all the lore of trailing learned in America that I must use on this day. Come." He stepped from the porch and set course for the stables.

"But who would do such a thing, Marcus?" Charles asked, following his friend. "Who would . . ." He hesitated as Marcus swung to meet his eyes. "Oh, by all that's holy! Do you believe that Prussian pig would have this as a method of revenge?"

"The thought did occur to me, Charles," Marcus admitted. "Come, let us hurry to the horses. If the lady of luck is with us, we may yet have time to catch up with them before injury is done to Penny." Marcus broke into a run and came to the stables as Jolin led three sleek mounts to the yard. Without another word, he took the reins of one of the horses and threw himself into the saddle. He was off and away before Charles could gain the saddle.

* * *

Marcus had located the point of abduction and halted by the time Charles arrived at the spot. Behind the younger man came the earl and Robroy.

"What is it you make of the scene, Marcus?" Charles asked, stepping to the ground.

Kneeling to study the tracks in the road, Marcus shook his head, saying, "There's little to be read here, my friend. 'Tis evidence of a struggle at the roadside. From the look of it, I judge it to be two or three men who have performed this act." He was silent for a moment, his finger tracing a spot in the dirt of the road. "Ah, hah!" he exclaimed suddenly as he moved forward and again dropped to one knee to trace an indentation in the road surface. It was at that moment the earl and his eldest son dismounted from lathered horses.

"What is it, Marcus?" the earl asked.

Marcus stood and faced him. " 'Tis news of the worst sort, I fear, my lord. From the appearances about this spot, an abduction has taken place." He swung his glance to Charles. "Come, friend. Take notice of the irregular mark of the blacksmith's weld left in the dust by the rim of some carriage. It seems to me that, since there has been none other along this way, it may well be the carriage in which our Penelope is prisoner." He mounted his horse adding, "Return to the halls, my lord Earl. Contact the authorities and await word from Penny, in the event I have guessed wrong." Then he set out along the road, with Charles hard on his heels.

CHAPTER THIRTEEN

The heat of midday engulfed the darkened room where Penelope and the abigail remained imprisoned. Their search for a method of escape had given them little hope. It was with a heavy sigh that Becky said, "I fear we are done, m'lady. 'Tis the will of whoever our captor might be to which we must bow."

"Nonsense," Penelope snapped. "You would just submit to the wishes of these vile men?"

"But, m'lady . . ."

"Nay, Becky. Whatever the identity of our abductor, he shall know the force of my anger and that of the Rothschilds."

"But, m'lady, how shall your family discover our whereabouts?"

Penelope smiled wryly. "Marcus will again aid the Rothschilds in their problems. I sense he will know what is to be done." She shook her head sadly. " 'Tis a pity. He does spend much of his time and efforts removing me from harm's way, only to ignore that which I suspect to be plain on my face."

"Is there nothing we might do, m'lady?" Becky asked.

Penelope was thoughtful a long moment before

getting to her feet. "The boards covering the window contain spaces between them. Quickly, Becky, your petticoat. A strip of the material, if you will. 'Tis a beacon I would present to the eye of any searchers, should they indeed find their way to this point."

With only a glance of curiosity, the maid bent to tear a streamer of material from the hem of her petticoat. Handing it to her mistress, she asked, "And what shall you do with this, m'lady?"

"Come," Penelope ordered, crossing to the window. Once there, she drew the drape, saying, "Hold the drape, Becky, that I might force the petticoat banner through a crack. Lord, allow that it be seen by those who are even now, I'm certain, searching for us."

Becky smiled weakly. "Do you think that it will be noticed at all? We do not even know our location. Is it not possible that we are in chambers facing away from the main travel of the road?"

"'Tis possible," Penelope agreed, working feverishly to force the strip of material through the narrow slot between the boards. "But, if memory serves me, 'twas to the right the carriage turned when we came to this place from the main road, and if that is correct, we are at the front of this place, facing the road." She hesitated, then added, "'Tis but a chance, Becky. We must do with such as we have."

"Aye, m'lady. Such as we have. 'Twould seem we have naught but a sliver of chance at regaining our freedom."

Completing the job of the cloth and shutters, Penelope turned to face the concerned abigail. "Faith, Becky. Retain the faith in those who love us. They shall not fail."

As Becky released her hold on the drapery, the sound of the bar being lifted from the door came to them. Their eyes met, each allowing to the other the fear they felt.

"Oh, m'lady," Becky exclaimed as the door swung inward.

"Courage," Penelope whispered. Then her eyes widened as the obese form at the doorway became recognizable. "Baron Von Lentin!" she gasped.

The Prussian gave her a bow of mockery, his lips stretched into a bitter smile. "My Lady Rothschild, I trust you find your surroundings comfortable."

Instant anger swept all other emotion from her. Leaving Becky's side, she advanced to within two paces of the Prussian. "Oh, you toad," she stammered in her anger. "Have you taken leave of your senses to perform such a deed as has been done this day?"

She was not aware of his movement until the palm struck her across the cheek, driving her to her knees on the stones of the floor.

"Silence," the baron growled. "'Tis respect you shall learn from this day hence, my lady, else you will suffer the more for stubbornness."

"M'lady," Becky moaned, running to her mistress.

From behind the baron stepped two of the men they had seen during the abduction. "What would you do with us, my lord?" asked the larger of the two.

"Prepare *her* for passage," the Prussian ordered, indicating Penelope.

"No, do not lay hands on her," Becky ordered, standing to shield Penelope with her own body.

In one step, the baron was in front of her. His hand struck again and the abigail dropped to the stones.

"Take her," the Prussian ordered, stepping back.

Rough hands gripped Penelope before she could move from their reach. She was pulled to her feet and held while her hands were again tied.

"Now," the baron ordered, "to the carriage with her. Draw the curtain lest she be noticed."

"Aye, your lordship," came the answer. "And what of this one?"

"Leave her. She shall remain here until I am free of the stench of this soil."

"Oh, by the saints," Becky begged. "Allow me to accompany my lady. I shall—"

The hand struck again, jarring Becky from her feet. She was aware of the door closing and the bolt slipping home, then she was alone in the chamber. Her senses swam as she made to rise. Then an engulfing blackness took her.

Charles and Marcus had followed the trail of the irregular wheel rim for several miles when Marcus asked, "Do we near the baron's estate, Charles?"

The question brought a puzzled expression to the younger man's face. "It is possible that we are wrong in our suspicions, Marcus. 'Tis possible the baron had nothing to do with this thing."

Marcus slowed his steed. "What brings such a chance to your mind at this time, Charles? Have you recalled another who would do such a thing?"

"No, no other. But the baron's estate is not in this direction. If, indeed, Pen is within the carriage that made these tracks, it is not to the Prussian she is being taken."

"We shall see," Marcus said. " 'Tis possible, you'll admit, the man arranged another site for her imprisonment." He again turned to the tracks. "Come, we gain nothing by this. It is of little matter who perpetrated the thing; it has been done. We must make haste to undo it."

Minutes later they came to a crossroad and dismounted to pick the proper track from among several which had been laid down. Striding some twenty paces along the road they had been following, Marcus halted, saying. "No. 'Tis not here." He retraced his steps and moved left along the crossroad. Suddenly he dropped to a knee to study a track. When he stood from his inspection, he smiled at Charles. "'Tis the weld mark. Come."

With the direction known to them, there was little need to watch the tracks. They pushed their mounts at top speed along the road.

Half an hour later they drew to the side to allow a fast-moving black carriage drawn by black steeds to pass; then they were again on their way. Another mile along the road they sighted the remains of what once had been a proud country house. Marcus slowed his steed and cast an eye to the tracks of the road.

"Hold, Charles," he ordered. "It seems our search ends at the ruin there. The carriage must have turned. Come, let us investigate."

"The black carriage which sped past us, Marcus?" Charles asked.

"Aye, I'll wager it was that one. Let us pray our Penny is within those walls. Come, let us use stealth in our approach, lest a guard awaits us."

So saying, he let his mount move forward slowly until he was within fifty feet of the house. Then, dismounting, he signaled to his companion, and together they made their way to the entrance.

"Marcus," Charles whispered, pointing to a strip of white cloth which hung from a slot of the shutters.

Marcus nodded, answering, "'Tis too clean and white to have been there long, my friend. Perhaps it was put there as a beacon to catch a searcher's eye. Come." He slipped inside the entrance, his glance swinging to cover all corners. He spotted a door to his right and moved quickly to unbar it.

"Use caution, Marcus," Charles warned as the bar was freed.

Marcus swung the door open and, after a moment, stepped inside. A moment later, he called, "Come, Charles. 'Tis Becky. Assist me to move her."

Together they carried the unconscious girl from the

chamber and laid her on the ground. After a brief inspection, Marcus said, "Water, my friend. 'Tis all that is needed to bring her around."

Without a word, Charles turned and made his way to the rear of the house. Minutes later he returned with a hollow gourd full of water. " 'Tis foul water, I fear, Marcus. A cleaning would aid the well."

"No matter," Marcus answered, taking the gourd from him. " 'Tis moisture." So saying, he sprinkled the unconscious girl's face with the water. Minutes later she moaned slightly and opened her eyes.

She stared up at Marcus for a long moment. Then, suddenly, her eyes opened wide and she gasped, "Oh, my lord, Lady Penelope. They have her!"

"Who has her, lass?" Marcus asked, assisting her to a sitting position.

"The one she so detests. The baron. He and others took her from this place, leaving me behind."

"The carriage," Marcus asked. "Can you describe it?"

She shook her head and passed a hand over the abrasion on her cheek left by the hand of the Prussian. "Black it was, my lord. All black."

"Aye," Charles said. " 'Twas the one we thought, Marcus. Even now Pen is being whisked from us to God knows where. We must hurry."

Marcus was on his feet, already moving toward the mounts. "Stay with the lass, Charles," he ordered. " 'Tis your help she'll be needing. I'll see to Penny." Then he was in the saddle and away.

Upon her return to the carriage by the pockmarked driver, Penelope was placed in a seat and ordered to remain quiet. Moments later the Prussian and the three abductors entered the carriage and took seats. The carriage door had barely swung shut when the vehicle was in motion.

"A good day's work, is it not, my lady?" the baron asked.

"My family will surely see you punished for your actions," Penelope answered.

His expression darkened at the words. "The family Rothschild frightens me not at all, my lady. 'Tis a Prussian officer they have angered. They'll find me not as the sniveling Englishmen to confront."

Penelope laughed bitterly at the words. "And was it a sniveling Englishman who allowed you your Prussian life, my lord?"

The statement earned her another vicious slap across her cheek. The abrasion left by the baron's hand stood out in the dim light of the curtained carriage.

"No need for that, guvnor," one of the thugs said. "The lass's hands are tied."

"You will remain silent," the Prussian ordered. "I pay you not for your opinion."

An expression of concern came over the abductor's features at the order. "And is it wife you'll be making of the lass, guvnor?"

"Never," Penelope snarled. "Never will I allow myself to be wed to such a pig."

The Prussian's eyes hardened on her for a moment. Then suddenly his lips stretched into a smile which sent chills of ice over Penelope. "The decision as to that has not been made as yet," he said. " 'Tis possible upon arrival in my native land that I shall transform this lady of the English courts into a willing and passionate serving girl." He laughed heartily. "There are others of noble Prussian birth who, as friends of mine, would enjoy such a one as this at their call."

"Marcus will kill you," Penelope stated, the meaning behind his words shocking her senses.

"Ah, yes, the Duke of Barrington," the Prussian chuckled. "It will be my pleasure to afford him information of your fate once we reach Prussia." His eyes narrowed. "And is it this English fop of a duke you prefer to one such as myself?"

"Any would be preferable to one such as you," she answered bitterly.

"Oh, your pardon, guvner," one of the abductors interrupted, "would this duke she speaks of be after revenging her fate?"

The Prussian fixed the man with a glance of disdain. "You fear a man because of his title? You Englishmen are all of an accord."

"Marcus will come," Penelope said. "He will come for me and all of you will know his wrath."

"Hah!" the Prussian snapped. "The man is a dolt." The carriage slowed at that moment, bringing a puzzled expression to the faces of the men within. Drawing back a curtain, the baron called to the driver, "What is about? Why do we slow?"

"A rider approaches at a run, my lord," was the answer.

Drawing the side curtain further back, the Prussian looked out and a moment later hastily drew the curtain into place again. "Blast!" he said, then loudly ordered, "Apply the whip to those horses."

In that brief moment before the curtain fell back into place, Penelope glimpsed the horseman; Marcus's features were unmistakable. Her heart pounded in her breast as hope sprung alive. She opened her mouth to scream as the hoofbeats of the passing steed drew abreast, but a hand of steel clamped over her lips, preventing sound from emitting.

When the rider had passed to the rear of the racing coach, the Prussian removed his hand from her mouth, saying, "Would you warn your lover, Rothschild slut? I think not. Take note of our numbers lest you lead your chosen to his death."

She faced him with burning eyes. " 'Twas Marcus, Baron. I think it is your party which shall know suffering before long."

"By your pardon, my lord," one of the ruffians said. " 'Twas not mentioned in our contract that we should endanger our lives. If this duke the lass mentions is here, it strikes me that we could all of us be in danger."

"Is it cowards I've hired?" the baron snarled.

The three men were unabashed by his words. "No," the speaker said, "not cowards, my lord, but men who would receive just due for their labors."

"Oh, it is your just due you shall receive at the hands of Marcus," Penelope snapped before the Prussian could answer. "He shall have the lives of all of you or I miss my guess."

"Silence, wench," the baron growled. Then, to the men, "You shall be paid for your labor, make no error of it. I shall pay you well when we are aboard the ship."

A moment's silence followed the statement, during which the three exchanged glances. Finally the previous speaker said, "We would be having the pay now, my lord, before we travel further."

The Prussian reddened at the words. "Is there no trust in any Englishmen, then?" he demanded.

The question brought a chuckle from one of the bandits. "No, not in the likes of us, my lord. 'Tis not trust we depend on, but the coin of the realm. 'Tis all the trust we shall ever need, I'm thinking."

Angered, the Prussian sent his glance around at the three faces. "And what are your demands for this bit of extra labor which you suspect might be visited upon you?"

"A moment," the speaker said, bending to converse in whispers with his comrades. After some moments of discussion, he eyed the baron, saying, " 'Tis double we shall have, my lord. Else we shall not continue with this thing."

"Double?" the baron gasped. "Are you mad? The

pay you have already received is outrageous. I shall pay half again and no more."

The ruffian nodded. "So be it, my lord." He turned to his companions. "Call for the carriage to stop. I would be done with this."

When the curtain had been drawn back and the man had prepared to do as ordered, the baron snapped, "Very well. You shall have your double payment. Half now and half when we are delivered aboard the ship."

The leader of the thugs eyed his men and, receiving their nods, said, "As you wish, my lord." He extended a hand toward the Prussian for payment.

" 'Tis money you shall not live to spend," Penelope said as the baron opened his pocketbook and extracted the amount.

The leader smiled at her, saying, " 'Tis without life your fancy will be should he attempt to best the group of us, lass."

"Even now the shadows lengthen. Do you think any man can follow in the dark?" the baron taunted, leering at Penelope.

The thug shrugged. " 'Tis better I will feel, my lord, when we are into the city and through it. I would have the traffic of many carriages about us."

"That will arrive with the darkness," the baron said. "And once through the city, we shall meet the ship I have prepared." His glance swung to Penelope. "At the midnight hour, we shall set sail for the continent, and your duke will find his efforts to no avail."

"Never will my family or Marcus cease hunting you," she answered with more certainty than she felt. A glance at the opening between curtain and carriage frame showed her that evening was indeed drawing near. Her heart sank when she realized the futility of any search after dark.

Something in her expression seemed to allow the Prussian to read her inner thoughts. He laughed heartily. "The enthusiasm with which you speak seems to be waning, my English lady. Resign yourself. There is naught your family or your duke can do to assist you now. You are mine to do with as I wish."

Her jawline stiffened. "It may be that you will do with me as you wish, Baron, but I shall never, in this life or any other, be yours." She turned her head to the side so she would not be forced to look at him.

"Your manner will change in time. You shall become a fine baroness, else you become a harlot of a servant girl." He laughed loudly at his statements.

"It shall be neither," she said, without facing him. " 'Tis you who shall pay a price for this day's doings."

"We shall see, lass. We shall see." Turning to the ruffian leader, he ordered, "Advise the driver that he should slow when we enter the city, lest we attract undue attention."

"He is not without common brains, my lord," was the answer. "He shall take us through with no question from any."

From that moment on, there was little said. Only on the occasion of a particularly rough stretch of road was comment made. Then full darkness fell upon the land, and Penelope's hopes fell with it.

"I am lost," she told herself, "for even the most dedicated of men could not follow now."

CHAPTER FOURTEEN

Flaying his steed for every ounce of speed it could muster, Marcus cursed the falling darkness as he made his way along the road in pursuit of the carriage holding Penelope. He was aware of the animal's labored breathing, and realized the creature had given its all. Drawing to a stop, he dismounted and for a short while—until impatience ruled him—walked, leading the animal at a slow pace.

Full darkness had fallen when he again swung into the saddle, saying, "Come, noble beast, 'tis to the city we must turn. There is no tracking the carriage in this light." He heeled the animal into motion and it moved at an ungainly trot, the day's efforts apparent in its every breath.

It was fully an hour later when he drew the animal to a stop at the front gate of an elaborate townhouse. Dismounting, he made his way through the gate to the stoop of the house and worked the iron knocker. Only moments following his knock, the door was opened by a servant holding a candle high to peer out into the darkness.

" 'Tis the Duke of Barrington," Marcus announced. "I would have words with the viscount."

The servant ushered him into the foyer and, with a word and a bow, left him. Seconds later the old viscount came toward him, saying, "My lord. To what does this humble house owe such a pleasure?"

" 'Tis information and your assistance I am in need of this night, old friend," Marcus answered.

"If 'tis mine, then surely it is yours. But come, you appear at the point of exhaustion. Come. Some wine will help."

"There is no time, I fear. Penelope, the daughter of Earl Rothschild, is in the hands of the Prussian devil."

"Eh, what? Do you suggest what I believe you do?"

Marcus nodded. "Aye. He has abducted her. I have half-killed a mount this day and am in need of another."

"But where are you going? 'Tis dark beyond seeing. How—"

"Earlier you brought news of the baron's going from these shores. You made mention of his arrangements for the voyage. Did you also learn from which point he was to sail?"

The viscount was thoughtful for a moment before saying, "No. But 'tis of no concern. We shall have the information momentarily." So saying, he called to a servant and gave the man instructions. When the servant had gone from the house, the old man turned back to Marcus, saying, "Now, 'tis food and drink you shall have. There is naught to be done until my man returns with the information. I would, in the meantime, have the tale of what has passed."

Reluctantly, Marcus admitted the truth of the words. He allowed the viscount to lead him to a small dining room and accepted a measure of wine. When food had been called for and brought, he recalled the events of the day for the old man.

When he finished, the viscount studied him for a

long moment before asking, "And the portion you have omitted, my friend?"

Puzzled, Marcus shook his head. "I have omitted nothing to my knowledge, sir. To what do you make reference?"

"Is it possible then that you do not admit to yourself the change in your feelings since your first meeting with the Penelope lass?" he laughed. " 'Tis unlike you to refuse your own counsel, Marcus. Do you blind yourself to personal emotions?"

A smile came to Marcus's lips. He shook his head in negative answer. "No, my thought-discerning friend, I do not ignore my sympathies. 'Twas not known to me that my love of the lass was so apparent to those around me. 'Tis she I would take for wife, when she is again safe."

"And have you spoken of such to Rothschild?"

"I have. He is not opposed to such a joining."

This brought a loud, raucous laugh from the old man. "Not opposed, you say? Not opposed? Aye, 'tis my thought he welcomes you with open arms. It will be a fine match for all concerned."

"My thanks, my lord. Your feelings concerning this, matter much to me."

"Does this then mean you have chosen to give up your America and remain in England?"

Marcus nodded. "It is necessary that I return to America for a short time to handle some affairs of importance. Then I shall return to England and become the duke my father wished me to become."

"Ah, good. Good," the old one said, pleased at the revelation. " 'Tis a day to—"

He broke off as the servant returned and entered the dining hall. "Well, come, man, the information we seek. What of the baron's whereabouts?"

" 'Tis said he made hire of a small sailing craft from the brothers Rolfe, my lord," the servant answered. "The elder of the brothers even now sails to meet the baron and his party at a designated site."

"And what of this site, man? Speak quickly."

The servant bowed. " 'Tis not known, my lord. 'Twas said the other brother would know of the vessel's whereabouts. I had no opportunity to speak to him of it, he being gone for the evening's sport at the grog shop known as the Green Frog."

The viscount turned to Marcus. " 'Tis acquainted I am with this grog shop frequented by such as he, Marcus. Come, I will accompany you. We will locate this Rolfe person and speak with him of his brother's whereabouts."

Marcus nodded and the two of them turned to leave. They were halted by the servant saying, "Beg pardon, my lord. The Rolfe brothers are well known for their smuggling activities. It is little you shall learn from either of them as to the other."

The viscount was thoughtful for a moment, then crossed to a cabinet and withdrew a brace of pistols. Handing one of the weapons to Marcus, he said, " 'Tis of an age I am to brook no reluctance from one such as this Rolfe. Come, Marcus, we shall find this man and acquire the information you seek."

Accepting the pistol, Marcus smiled at the older man's determination. "Lead on, old friend. Between the two of us, the man will tell all he knows."

It was near ten when they entered the Green Frog in the lower portions of the city. From every direction, the stench of human bodies and soured drink assailed their nostrils. The dregs of the kingdom were at every table and lined the bar. To a man, they turned to fix the two newcomers with glances of disdain.

" 'Tis a pleasant group we visit," the viscount said, his eyes swinging to take in the room. "On your guard, Marcus, lest one or more amongst them thinks of our purses as his own."

"Aye," Marcus agreed. " 'Tis our wits we'll need

this night should any turn his hand against us in this place."

Approaching the bar, the viscount signaled to the churlish bartender. "Grog, if you will, my good man," he called.

When the man placed the pints before them and accepted payment, the viscount said, " 'Tis told that a body could find means of quietly departing the country in this place. Such interests me."

The bartender fixed him with jaundiced eye. "Aye, and is it the law you are, sir? For there is no such occurrence as you suggest in this establishment."

Marcus moved to the far side of the viscount to a point where the wall was at his right. Quietly he drew the pistol from under his coat and placed the muzzle on the lip of the bar. The bore was aimed directly at the heart of the bartender.

"Face me, slowly," he ordered, his body shielding the weapon from the sight of those others in the room. The man turned to face him, an angry retort on his lips for one who would speak in such a way. His eyes widened as they settled on the muzzle of the pistol. His hands left the bar to drop below the surface.

"If you move further or call out, I shall drop flint and put a ball in your head," Marcus said softly. "The bandage on my head covers the furrow of a bullet. That furrow claws at my nerves. Add not to my condition, lest you lose your life."

The viscount laughed. "Ah, well done, Marcus. 'Twas little he would have done for us through normal means." He faced the unmoving bartender. "Now, my good man, we would speak with one called Rolfe. Of the smuggling persuasion he is. Point him out to us."

The man's head shook. "There is none of that name here, my lord."

"But you do know the man," Marcus said.

"No, guvnor. The name has never been heard by me."

" 'Tis a pity to have to kill such a one as this, Marcus," the viscount said. "But he would lie to us. Come. Put a ball in him and let us leave this place." So saying, he too drew a pistol and, turning to conceal the action, drew the flint back to full cock. The eye of the bore was steady on the bartender. "Do you think we jest, dolt? We would have this Rolfe person, or your life. And it is none would miss the likes of you, I think."

Threatened by two as seemingly determined as these, the man jerked his head to the side, saying, "The table near the wall. 'Tis the yellow-haired one you seek."

"Call to him," Marcus ordered.

The man hesitated, his eyes meeting Marcus's, then dropping to look into the gaping throats of the gun muzzles. Finally he turned, calling, "Nigel, a word with you over here."

The blond-haired man turned, studied the bartender a moment, then got to his feet and moved to the bar. "Now if it is my bill you are again to mention, 'tis as I said, I will . . ."

"Silence!" the viscount ordered, turning his pistol to center it on the man's chest. " 'Tis information concerning the whereabouts of your brother we would have."

"I have no brother," the man snarled. " 'Tis unseemly for strangers to place weapons on a man who has done naught to deserve such."

"Ho! What's amiss?" came a cry from the side of the room as the viscount's pistol was noticed. No sooner had the question been voiced than men were on their feet throughout the shop.

"As you stand!" Marcus yelled, placing his pistol to the head of the bartender. "Should any move toward us, the two under our guns die in their spots."

"Stay!" the frightened bartender cried. " 'Tis of no concern to any but the gentlemen and Nigel."

"Wisely said," the viscount laughed. "Now, Nigel, your brother. Where is he bound for? Waste not our time or you shall meet death this very night."

The smuggler hesitated a moment, his glance going to Marcus's face. Something in the set of that face sent a visible shudder across him.

"We'll not abide your hesitation, man," Marcus said. "What is it to be, your life or the location of your brother's meeting with the Prussian?"

"My lords," the man began, his voice becoming a whine, "what is it my brother has done to bring the fury of two such as you down upon his head? We are but simple seamen. We—"

"Are smugglers and worse, I'd wager," the viscount snapped. "Idiot, we care not about your brother. Our concern is for the passenger he carries this night. Now, quickly, where do we locate him?"

Again the man's eyes swept over the gathering. "In truth, sir, there is nothing of my brother you would have?"

"Nothing," the viscount assured him. "Make haste, man. I tire of this." The pistol came up to center on the man's nose.

"Aye, my lord," the blond said, his hands coming up as if to stop the ball in flight. " 'Tis at Grovesnor Point my brother is to meet his cargo on this night."

"At what hour?" Marcus demanded.

"At midnight, my lord," the smuggler answered without hesitation. " 'Tis nothing illegal we do, sirs. 'Tis an honest night's work."

" 'Tis a word you have not the meaning of in your system," the old viscount snapped. "Marcus, shall we be gone?"

"In all haste, my friend," Marcus agreed. "The hour is even now drawing near. Come." Lowering the pistol from the head of the bartender, he swung it to cover the gathering. "My friend—the old one here—and myself shall leave this place now. Should any here desire to bring halt to our movement or follow in our path, know this: The balls in these two pistols care not which body they burn into." With the threat hanging in the odor-laden air of the place, he moved beside the viscount to the doorway.

At the door, the viscount swung around, the pistol steady in his hand. "'Twas any ten of such I could master in my youth," he said. "Out, Marcus, and ready the horses. I shall be certain of the hesitation of this group." With those words, he fished a purse from his pocket with his free hand and flung it toward the bar. "Drinks for all for as long as the coin therein lasts," he called. Then he swung through the door and, with Marcus's assistance, mounted.

"Well done, old friend," Marcus said, when none made to follow them. "'Twould seem there is little your years have done to slow you."

"'Tis as your father would say, and I'm certain you recall, 'It is not the years but the miles a man travels which age him.'"

Mounting his own steed, Marcus said, "I would have instructions on the route to this Grovesnor Point."

"I shall guide you, Marcus. Come."

"No, my lord, 'tis much you have done and even more you must do if things are to go as we wish. I would ask you to make contact with the authorities and have them join me as soon as possible. And would you send word of what is about to the Rothschilds?"

"Of course," the viscount agreed. Raising a hand, he pointed to the outskirts of the city. "'Tis a fast hour's ride you must make, Marcus. This Grovesnor Point is beyond Gravesend, so you'd best make haste. 'Tis the fire at the point you'll notice before you arrive. There will be no mistaking it, for there are none who would attempt landing without a beacon to guide them. I shall do as you've asked." So saying, he turned his mount and, with a wave of his hand, went at a gallop along the streets.

Behind him, Marcus applied heels to his own horse and charged off in the direction indicated by the viscount. "Lord, be with my endeavors this night," he muttered in prayer as the wind swept around him.

CHAPTER FIFTEEN

The long days of ministering to Marcus and the equally arduous day just passed taking her strength, Penelope awoke from a fitful sleep as the coach was drawn to a halt. The smell of the sea was in the air and the coolness which accompanied it brought a shiver to her body as she fought to realize where she was.

"Quickly," the Prussian ordered. "To the point. The craft should soon come within sight."

The order and the harsh voice brought the events of the day back to her with painful clarity. The attempted movement she made with her hands reminded her they were bound and of little use to her. Then a rough hand gripped her arm in the darkness, and she was pulled from her position on the carriage seat.

"Come, you," the baron ordered. " 'Tis your last few steps on English soil you shall take at this time. Remember them well, for you'll not be returning."

She was pulled from the coach, missed the step and fell headlong into the rock and dirt of the beach. A cry of pain escaped her as her weight came to bear on her imprisoned arms. Then she was dragged to her feet and pulled unceremoniously across the beach toward the sea.

"Quickly," the baron called to the driver of the carriage. "Assist them in finding wood for the signal fire. The hour of our departure draws near."

"Aye, my lord," the pockmarked one answered, getting from his perch to make his way down the beach in search of driftwood.

With the others away from them, the Prussian turned to Penelope. "Now, my lady of the court, face your husband-to-be and allow him the privilege of your lips on his."

"Never," Penelope snarled, pulling back as far as his grip would allow. "I would rather die first."

With one vicious jerk, he pulled her against him and pushed his mouth hard on hers. She fought with all her might. Suddenly, angered by her actions, he swung a fist to her jaw, saying, "I shall tame you, my pretty. Fear not."

The blow caught her squarely. Blackness swept over her and she collapsed, held up only by his grip on her bound wrists.

With an exclamation of disgust, he released his hold on her and allowed her unconscious body to drop to the sand. Then, cursing into the wind, he screamed at the men to hurry with the wood.

" 'Tis not a simple thing to find in the dark, my lord," one of them called back. " 'Twill require a bit of time to gather the amount needed for our job this night."

With a glance at the still-unconscious girl, the Prussian stomped off down the beach mumbling curses at the four men as he went. Suddenly he bent to snatch a bit of wood from the sand. "And what is it you would call this, you dolts," he screamed. "Search not for the perfect log. 'Tis only something to burn we require."

Behind the raging baron, Penelope's eyes fluttered

and opened. She lay for a moment, the pain in her head forcing all else from her mind. Then an awareness of what had happened flooded over her and she was immediately frightened. She next heard the growling voice of her captor some yards distant, and as quietly as possible rolled to her knees. Getting her feet under her, she turned in the opposite direction from the voices and began running as best her bound hands and bruised body would allow. It was only moments later when she heard the startled cry of the Prussian.

"All of you! Come quickly! The wench has taken herself down the beach at a run. Come, we must catch her."

The words lent speed to her feet and she fairly flew along the sand, a prayer for salvation on her lips. Suddenly she ran headlong into a pile of driftwood and went over it onto the sand. Stunned, she lay for a moment without moving. Then, with a shake of her head to clear it, she spit sand from her mouth and again got to her feet. It was then she realized the fall had cost her her freedom.

With a heavy sigh flowing from his chest, the pock-marked driver reached to clutch her wrist. "Here, my lord," he yelled between heavy breaths. " 'Tis over here the lass is."

In seconds, the group was around her. The baron was the last to arrive at the spot. He breathed in heavy gasps as he faced her, just inches away in the darkness. His hand came out of the dark to deliver an open-handed slap across her face. "Wench," he snarled, "think you to escape me? Know it now, I shall see you dead before I allow any other to have you. Now, back to the point." To the men he snarled, "Quickly. The firewood. The time of departure draws near."

A hoarse chuckle left the lips of the driver. " 'Tis a good bit of assistance the lass has furnished us in that vein, my lord. For 'twas a handsome pile of drift-wood that caused her to lose her feet and go headlong into the sand. 'Tis my thought we've aplenty for the fire we shall need this night."

The baron laughed loudly at the statement. Then, with a jerk on the girl's arm, he said, "It is our thanks you have, lady. Now come. You'll not be free of my grip until you are aboard the vessel." He led her down the beach to the point of land where the ship would shortly arrive.

"You are detestable," she panted. "Marcus will—"

"Never lay eyes on you again," he finished for her. Shaking her roughly, he pointed out to sea. "Set it well in your head, Lady Rothschild. Your future lies across yon waters. 'Twould be your best fortune to make the best of what your lot is to be."

"Does it not occur to you, Prussian fool, that Marcus is a man of such courage that he will dog you wherever you may take me?" she demanded.

He laughed heartily at that. In the midst of his laughter, the crackling light of the fire leaped toward the sky. "In but a short time, the winds will carry us to Ostende on the Belgium coast. Your duke, in the way of all Englishmen, shall assume all are stupid as he. Should he arrive here, he will imagine us bound for the French coast."

She was about to retort when the coach driver called, "My Lord. 'Tis the ship. I see the light. 'Tis even now drawing near."

All eyes swung out to sea. There in the darkness could be seen the swinging lantern of a ship's prow. Moments later the sounds of a boat being launched came through the night stillness, and other lanterns were visible as the oarsman lowered himself into the small craft.

The Prussian chuckled wickedly. "Now, my lass, where is this saviour of yours who is to do me vile?

Can it be possible the Englishman realizes he has met his match and deems it wise to forgo the day to Prussian superiority?"

"Ho, the land," came the call from the sea. "Make ready to receive a line."

Instantly the coach driver ran to the point, and moments later a line was cast in and the boat slid up on the beach. From the stern of the vessel, a man six feet tall stepped out and crossed to the baron. " 'Tis away from these shores I would be as soon as humanly possible, my lord. The tides here are of such to cause any seaman concern."

"There is no need for concern," the Prussian answered. "My lady and myself are even now prepared to board your ship."

The sailor's eyes shifted to Penelope. He stepped forward the better to see her in the light cast by the fire's glow. Suddenly he faced the baron again. "The lass's hands are tied. Is it an abduction you are performing?"

" 'Tis none of your concern," the Prussian snarled. "You have been paid to carry us to the shores of Belgium."

Penelope stepped a pace toward the seaman saying, "Oh, sir, 'tis captive I am. Even now my family and friends are in pursuit of this Prussian pig. I beg you—"

The Prussian swung a flat hand to her cheek, snarling, "Enough, wench." He returned his attention to the seaman. "Well, sir, we have a contract."

"Aye, we do that," was the answer. "But for a voyage, not for abduction of such a lass. 'Tis over much you presume, my lord. I'll have no part in it." He turned away as if to return to the boat.

"I have paid you a fair amount," the baron growled.

"Aye, for a voyage to the shores of Belgium. Not for such as you ask now, though."

Anger was apparent in the Prussian's voice when

he asked, "Very well, what is your price for such a thing?"

" 'Tis a crime you ask me to aid you in, my lord," the sailor answered. " 'Twould be unseemly for respectable seamen to be caught up in such a thing."

"Damn you!" the Prussian screamed. " 'Tis naught but more pay you hold for. Very well, I've said, what is your price?"

"The same plus half," was the growling answer. "And let not your tongue place over much of the acid on my person, my lord. The sea consumes everything that is dropped into its throat."

"I need none of your idle threats," the baron answered, withdrawing his purse from a pocket. He counted out the extra fee and handed it to the man. "Now, let us away from this place."

"Hold, my lord," the leader of the abductors said. " 'Tis the final portion of our pay we would have at this moment." He advanced toward the Prussian, his comrades at his side.

"Ah, so be it," the Prussian sighed, again opening his purse. " 'Tis my fate that no honest man is about on this day." He tendered the required amount to the abductors, saying, "Now take yourselves from this place. Speak naught of this, lest the weight of my vengeance come to rest on your necks." He turned away to clutch Penelope's hands and pull her toward the waiting boat.

"I shan't," she screamed, dragging back against his weight.

He turned to face her, saying, "Walk or be rendered unconscious and carried. 'Tis none of your antics I shall put up with this moment."

Anger coupled with fear swept over her. Without thought as to her danger, she spat in the Prussian's face, saying, " 'Tis dead I prefer to be than aboard yon ship with such as you."

He wiped at the spittle, his narrowed eyes burning

into hers. "As you will, my lady." Then he struck her a vicious blow and she again went to the sand of the beach.

"Here now, governor," she heard the seaman say as blackness took her.

Marcus entered Gravesend minutes before midnight. Moments later he was through the town and racing along the shoreline toward Grovesnor Point. Behind him, from a grog shop in Gravesend, several fishermen watched his passing.

" 'Tis urgent business yon rider is on, I'd say," one remarked.

"Aye. 'Tis fortunate he will be to arrive where he intends without breaking a horse's leg or his own neck."

With this wisdom spoken, they turned back to their drinks and their former discussion.

The horse breathed heavily as Marcus rounded a bend and came upon the fire. Sliding from the saddle, he ran forward, the pistol coming into his hand. The sound of voices slowed him to a stop behind the black carriage.

" 'Tis no matter what you choose to believe," someone said, " 'twas horse's hooves I heard."

"In this sand, such would be impossible. Your imagination will have its way with you," another voice snarled.

"Let us be gone from this place," the first voice said. "Our work is finished. Let us to Gravesend. The grog shop there is serving yet."

"Aye," a third member of the group added, " 'tis the taste of that Prussian I would rinse from my mouth. I think he'll find the Belgians less willing to please than the English."

"Aye," came an answer from the fourth member. " 'Tis none of his vicious tongue they'll brook. Come. Douse the flames and let us to the inn at Gravesend."

Marcus waited no longer. Silently he returned to his horse and mounted. Then, for the first several steps, he moved slowly lest the hoofbeats of his steed be heard and identified. When he was certain he was beyond earshot, he put the beast into a run back toward Gravesend.

There were but two men and the innkeeper about when he drew the steed to a stop and dismounted. Entering the grog shop, he sent an eye around the room before saying, "I am in need of honest Englishmen this night."

The three present had settled their attention on him at his entrance. Now they exchanged puzzled glances before the bartender asked, "And who might be asking for such, my lord?"

Marcus advanced to the bar. " 'Tis the Duke of Barrington I am. A carriage of deep black swept through your town earlier." He paused, his glance steady on the bartender.

That man nodded. "Aye, 'twas allowing none to slow it."

Marcus was aware of the two men from the table getting to their feet to move closer. "In that carriage," he continued, "was a lass of eighteen years. The daughter of Rothschild Halls she is. Accompanying her was a Prussian baron and the thugs who abducted her."

"To what purpose, my lord?" the smaller of the two men from the table asked.

"That the Prussian might take her to his homeland and force his will upon her," Marcus answered.

The anger at the information was apparent in the man's eyes. "And what is it you would have of these honest Englishmen, my lord?"

"Even now the abductors are on their return to this place to partake of the grog. I would have them held until the authorities of the crown arrive." He paused, then added, " 'Tis cutthroats they are and not to be taken lightly."

Without another question, the bartender said, "Off with you, Darcy. Collect the village guard." His glance centered on Marcus. "And of the lass, my lord? Is she safe?"

Marcus shook his head. "No. Even now she is aboard a smuggler's boat bound for an unknown port in Belgium. I would have a swift craft to overtake them. Is there such in Gravesend?"

The remaining customer of the grog shop asked, "Smuggler's boat, you say? And would it be Beekster or the Rolfe brothers you make reference to, my lord? For there are no others who make use of this coast with impunity."

" 'Tis one of the Rolfe brothers."

"Aye, then it is indeed a speedy craft you are in need of." He turned to the bartender. "And would he be needing the folly the Collingston lad toys with?"

"Are you daft, man?" the bartender asked. " 'Tis but a plaything. The open waters would see to it before a man could take breath."

"He claims not," was the retort. "And, low and swift as the Rolfe vessel is, there is no other could come near."

"Quickly," Marcus said. "What of this craft you mention? Where would a man find its owner?"

"He lives but a few steps from here," the bartender answered. "But, my lord, the craft is but a small thing overcrowded with sail. 'Tis in the lad that he will wager on its speed."

"Then I would have use of it, and of the lad, this night. Direct me, if you will."

"Concern yourself not, my lord," was the answer. "Harry will obtain the lad for you." He turned to the customer. "Make haste, Harry. Bring the lad from his bed. If the duke is of a mind to chance it, 'tis naught but right that he be allowed to."

When the man had left the building, the innkeeper asked, "Would you partake of drink, my lord?"

"Aye," Marcus said, drawing a purse from his pocket. "And for all who take part in the events of this night, the drink shall be paid for in full."

"The word is out," Darcy said, entering the pub. "The village guard is even now making to assemble here."

Hardly had the words been spoken when three younger men stepped into the inn, their eyes filled with the dregs of sleep. One of the three carried a musket. It was he who spoke. " 'Tis the far corner I shall occupy," he said, seeing to the flint of his weapon. "Once in, they shall not leave."

Within minutes, four more of the guard had arrived. The group occupied tables and stood at the bar with drinks before them, waiting. Moments later the sound of a carriage became evident to all present. There was a noticeable tensing in the room. Then the door swung inward and the men from the beach entered and made their way to the bar.

"Ah, 'tis grog I would be having," the pockmarked one said to the bartender. "Until the order is given to cease, man, we would drink of your product."

" 'Tis remaining with hands on the surface you shall be," Marcus announced, "lest your heads take leave of your shoulders from the musket at your back."

They froze in position for a moment, then cautiously turned to look at Marcus. "You make jest of us, my lord?" the pockmarked one asked.

" 'Tis the Duke of Barrington I am. Your actions this night shall earn you death should I fail to recover the lass you acquired for the Prussian."

The name had obvious impact on the four. Their eyes narrowed. "Come," said one to his comrades, "let us out of here before we are forced to deal with this dandy."

"Hold," the musket-bearer said from his corner. "One movement and 'twill be your last." The sound of the flint going to cock punctuated the words.

" 'Tis the destination of the Rolfe boat I will be having from you," Marcus ordered. "I would brook no lies from you." Drawing the pistol, he cocked it and aimed it at the pockmarked man. "I tire of waiting, pit-faced one. Answer."

The men exchanged glances. Then, with a shrug, the man answered, " 'Twas not death we bargained for with the Prussian. 'Tis to Ostende on the Belgium coast he travels."

At that moment, the man who'd gone for the boat owner stepped into the room accompanied by a yawning lad of twenty. "Aye," he exclaimed taking in the scene, "and it is caught the bustards are, is it? 'Tis a fine night's work we do." His glance met Marcus's. "Here is the lad of which I spoke."

"My lord," the boy said, " 'tis my craft you are in need of, I'm told."

"And your seamanship," Marcus answered. "The pay will be ample if you are able to overtake the ship of Rolfe and place me aboard."

The boy laughed. "The overtaking is no problem if he has only recently gone. For, speedy as his is, mine outraces the very wind. The boarding of his vessel will present a problem, I fear. Though it lies low in the water, 'tis still of a height beyond my craft."

"Hold," the innkeeper said. "There is a device which might serve." He went to a back room and moments later returned carrying a heavy line with a large hook attached to the end of it. " 'Tis the result of a joke perpetrated earlier on a boastful fisherman," he explained to Marcus. "Will it suffice?"

Marcus accepted the tool and studied it. "Aye,

'twill do nicely. 'Twas a whale the man was fishing for, I suspect."

The words brought laughter from all except the abductors. Turning to the boy, Marcus asked, "How quickly shall we make our departure, lad?"

The Collingston boy bowed and yawned. "The craft awaits, my lord. 'Tis wet we shall be before we overtake the Rolfe craft." He paused, his eyes widening slightly. " 'Twill be Rolfe and one other you face aboard the boat should you board her, my lord. 'Twill be overmuch for a single man to master."

"With the aid of my pistol, I shall attempt it, my friend. Come, let us hurry." He turned from the bar and, with a final glance at the abductors, said, "My thanks to all who have assisted me this night. 'Tis a fine thing you have done."

"Go with God, my lord," the barman said.

Minutes after leaving the tavern, Collingston led Marcus to a dock where a small sailboat of smooth lines and shallow draft was moored. Without a word, he dropped to the deck of the craft and turned to look up at the older man.

" 'Tis a small thing," Marcus said, stepping to the deck. " 'Tis more sail than any other."

"Aye, and faster than any in England. Come, my lord, assist me to apply the sail."

Once out of the harbor, the boy applied the cunning of his trade to the sail and the small craft fairly flew through the water. In no time, they swept past Grovesnor Point, where the Rolfe craft had landed to accept the Prussian and his captive.

"In only a short time, we shall be overtaking them, my lord."

"Aye," Marcus agreed, marveling at the speed of the craft. "Lord, let them have lights to be noticed, lest we pass them in the darkness."

Collingston laughed at the statement. "Have no

fear, my lord. 'Tis not a fool Rolfe is. He'd not chance collision with another in the sea lanes he travels."

Marcus, a silent prayer on his lips that the boy was right, settled himself to scan the sea ahead of them.

CHAPTER SIXTEEN

Penelope awoke to the sound of water lapping against wood and to the swell and toss of the sea. Darkness surrounded her, and the smell of resin and the sea were heavy in her nostrils. Her wrists ached from the binding which held them. Recalling the last moments ashore, when the Prussian had struck her, her heart sank and she wished for death. She lay on a pad in the bowels of the ship and, as she attempted to sit up, the ship rolled and she was tossed from the pad to the deck. The low moan of a snore came to her from only inches away. Holding her breath in fear lest she wake the sleeping one and bring the wrath of him down upon herself, she sobbed in silent despair as the ship moved across the waters, bound for Belgium.

"Oh, my Marcus," she thought, "I am lost. Lost forever to you. Oh, that God would this instant strike me dead."

Above her, the owner of the vessel guided the ship across the surface of the sea with only seamanship to guide him. The night was overcast; not a sliver of moon showed itself. Ahead of him, a lone deckhand worked at the sail as the wind carried the vessel eastward toward Belgium.

When the sails were to his liking, the deckhand came amidships to speak to his captain. " 'Tis a fair wind we ride tonight," he said.

"Aye," was the answer, "and a fair cargo we carry. The Prussian's taste in women is worthy of notice."

" 'Tis anything but proud I am of our task this night," the seaman said.

The captain laughed. " 'Tis the jingle of coin which shall bring the pride back into you when we deposit the baron and his lady on the shore of Belgium, I'm thinking. The bow watch is where you belong, is it not?"

"Aye. And 'tis there I go now. 'Twill be a long night for both of us."

"Go see to your lights, lest we collide with another on this pit-dark night."

Grumbling to himself, the seaman made his way forward, leaving the captain to his own thoughts.

Bow spray wet Marcus as the small craft slid silently over the surface of the sea. His eyes ached from the strain of searching for the telltale light of the larger craft which lay ahead of them, partaking of the same wind as they.

"We should be showing a light," the Collingston lad said.

"No," Marcus answered, " 'tis this darkness which shall accomplish what is done this night. I wish to give no warning to those we pursue."

"It was the midnight hour, you stated, when they drew anchor and made from Grovesnor Point?"

"It was."

"Then we should be within sight of the Rolfe vessel soon, my lord, for accounting for full sail, he could have gone little more than this distance in the time passed. Would you that I accompany you when you embark?"

A chuckle of appreciation escaped Marcus's lips.

"No, friend, but I thank you for the offer. 'Twill be enough if you will but place me aboard the vessel."

"I shall follow as best possible, my lord, until your luck is known to me."

Marcus was about to protest when he suddenly spied the flicker of light from a point to the right a distance ahead of them. "Look," he said. "Would that be the light of the vessel we seek?"

The small craft heeled around to aim directly at the wake of the other ship. "We shall know for certain in a moment, my lord."

"Is Rolfe's craft known to you?"

"Aye, and there will be no mistaking it even in this poor light. 'Tis quiet we should remain from this point, my lord. For sound does move easily across the waters. I shall make known to you if it truly is the ship we seek."

After what seemed a lifetime to Marcus, he heard the boy's whisper of identification from the stern. Immediately he swung around to say in low tones, "I shall go over the after section if possible."

"Aye," the lad whispered in answer, swinging the tiller slightly. "Prepare yourself."

Long minutes later the bow of the small vessel came under the overwhelming shadow of the larger craft. Without hesitation, Marcus swung the line and released the hook upward toward the deck of the Rolfe ship.

The contact of the hook with the surface of the other vessel seemed loud to his ears. Then he drew it back until it caught on the rail surrounding the main deck. With a final whispered word to the lad, he swung himself free and made his way, hand over hand, upward.

When his head came above the surface of the larger ship, he hesitated, his eyes searching each and every square foot of the deck as closely as possible in the darkness. Finally satisfied that none aboard was aware of his presence, he pulled himself upward and over the rail to fall softly to the deck boards.

He lay there for a moment regaining the breath which the climb had cost him. Then, getting to his feet, he moved toward the wheel area, pistol in hand.

When he was some ten feet from the wheel, the clouds of the sky suddenly slipped aside and allowed the moon to bathe the sea in whiteness. He hesitated momentarily, his eyes locked on the man who stood with wheel in hand, facing the bow. Then, with breath controlled, he again moved forward, his footsteps as light as those of a cat until he stood less than two feet from the man who steered the ship.

Raising the pistol to place it against the captain's head, he said, " 'Tis death you shall meet if you but move an eyelid, friend."

The man stiffened. He made as if to turn his head, thought better of it and asked, "By all that's holy, who might it be who places pistol to my head in the middle of an empty sea?"

" 'Tis the avenger who intends to take the life of a Rolfe should he cause a moment's problem," Marcus said with force. "Call your man forward."

" 'Tis piracy you perform, sir," Rolfe argued. "I think you take leave of your senses."

"Piracy it might be called, but 'tis naught compared to the abduction in which you are engaged. Call your man or I shall release the flint of my weapon."

After a long moment, the helmsman called to the hand who attended the bow watch. That person growled an answer and came amidships until he was within five feet of the wheel. Suddenly he stopped in his tracks. "What have we here?" he demanded.

"Silence," Marcus ordered, "else your captain loses his head and you join him. The cargo you carry toward Belgium shall not reach its destination. This craft will, at this moment, return to Grovesnor Point. It is by my order."

"And who might you be?" Rolfe asked.

"The Duke of Barrington and, at the moment, your commander, sir. Turn your ship or lose your life."

"Can you control such a vessel without assistance, sir?" Rolfe asked.

" 'Tis larger than this I've helmed," Marcus snarled. "You have no more time. Turn or I shall away with you and see to the return myself."

With a sigh of defeat, Rolfe nodded and swung the wheel. "See to the sail," he ordered as the ship heeled over in a tight turn. The seaman hesitated only a moment before turning to make his way forward again.

" 'Tis naught illegal I do on this night," Rolfe said when the seaman had gone.

"You have a Prussian and a lady aboard," Marcus countered.

"No, you mistake my cargo, my lord. 'Tis but a bit of contraband I carry this night. Would you deprive a man of a living?"

"Of his life, if he saw fit to lie a second time."

The ship owner was silent for a long moment before nodding. "Aye, the Prussian and his lady are below, sleeping the sleep of the innocent."

" 'Tis anything but the sleep of the innocent for the Prussian. He shall know my anger when we again rest off the point."

" 'Tis your lady he has?"

"Aye. And any mark upon her shall be exacted from those who assisted in her abduction."

The threat brought a long silence from Rolfe. Finally he said, "My lord, 'twas my intention to safeguard her. It was by my words alone she received only the one blow from the Prussian."

Anger swept over Marcus at the revelation. " 'Tis a long voyage you shall have this day, Rolfe, for you shall, when I deem, take this Prussian pig to the site he had previously arranged."

"You would release him and myself?"

"The man is heavy with purse. If he is aboard your ship when you return, I shall have your head."

Rolfe was thoughtful for a long moment, then he laughed. "Aye, my lord. There is little concern you should have of that. I think 'tis a short trip the fat one shall have. Short by much of the Belgium coast, I'd wager."

"Call to your man when the sail is correct. There is a lad in a small craft at our stern. I would have him aboard and his craft in tow."

Rolfe turned, ignoring the threatening pistol. "I would see the craft which overtook this vessel of mine. 'Twas not to my knowledge that such a one existed."

Marcus laughed bitterly. " 'Tis ever the way. Such as you deem yourselves above any other and therefore beyond catching. 'Tis the downfall of any who would perform such actions as you are involved in."

Below decks, unaware of the ship's new direction, Penelope sat where she'd been thrown from her pad. The rhythmic snores of the sleeping man were as needles to her senses. She was aware of footfalls on the deck above her and prayed silently that they would not awaken the Prussian.

Marcus still held the pistol on the captain of the ship when the lad of the swift boat came to the deck and crossed to him. "Yours shall be a bountiful reward for this night's work, my lad," he told the boy.

Rolfe turned at the words, his eyes going to the newcomer. "Aye, and it is the Collingston waif, is it? Now I understand my overtaking this night. And is it true as you'd guessed of your toy craft, lad?"

The boy nodded. "Aye, Rolfe, 'twas as I said. It does fairly skim the surface of the sea in its movement."

"That it must for you to have approached me in such short order. Ah, well. We must talk in the near future. I would have your ideas on increasing the speed of my vessel."

" 'Tis naught I shall do for such as you, Rolfe," Collingston answered. "The designs I apply myself toward are for the purposes of honest men."

The ship's captain laughed at the statement. "Well said. Then 'tis honest I shall become, if I must."

"As the leopard changes spots," Marcus said. "Attend to your course, man, lest you bring my anger to bear."

"Aye," Rolfe answered. " 'Tis a seaman I am and not of the sort to be needing directions on craft handling from the likes of you."

Marcus gave his attention to the boy. "And what of our landing at Grovesnor Point? Shall we need a fire beacon?"

"And a great one," Rolfe answered before the lad could speak. " 'Tis not to my liking to land at such a place at this hour. The tide has begun its course. 'Twill not be seemly for the lot of us should we go aground."

" 'Tis correct, he is," Collingston said. "Is it of necessity we return there, my lord?"

"No," Marcus answered. " 'Twas the point I had in mind, nothing else. Is there another site which will serve better?"

"Aye, my lord. 'Twould be Gravesend itself I would make for if it were my doing. For there is depth enough there for the draft of this vessel."

"Then Gravesend it is," Marcus said. "Even now the authorities of the crown should be arrived." He prodded the ship's captain with the pistol. "Set course for Gravesend, man."

The ship swung its bow slightly, and Rolfe said, " 'Tis a fine seaman you'll become one day, lad." Then his voice changed. "My lord, your mention of the crown's authorities does give me wonder if your word of earlier is for naught. Are you to place my ship and myself in irons?"

"I gave you my word, Rolfe," Marcus answered. " 'Tis your duty to see that your portion of the bargain is carried out. If such be the case, there's naught any will learn from me of your doings this night."

Rolfe laughed at the statement. "Oh, fear not, my lord, there will be little use I'll be having for the Prussian once his purse is no longer his. 'Tis a far swim he shall have this night."

Some time later Collingston said, "Ho, my lord, the lights of Gravesend. I think, from the lanterns visible, you were correct in your thought of the authorities."

Sending his glance shoreward, Marcus became aware of the pinpoints of light which moved from place to place around the docks of Gravesend. A sense of satisfaction swept over him as he said, "Rolfe, 'tis your longboat we shall be in need of if you are to remain unidentified."

" 'Tis yours for the asking," was the answer. "We come near recognition distance even now."

"Then send your man for the passengers this instant."

" 'Tis an unfriendly mood the Prussian will be in, I wager," Rolfe said. "His sort sets great store in having proper sleeping hours."

"His mood is of the least concern to me. Order your man to see to it. Order him to call to the baron first. I would have him on deck before the lass knows of our presence."

When the order had been given, Rolfe asked, "And is it death you plan to deal the Prussian before I have my promised chance, my lord?"

"No. Not by my hand," Marcus answered. "I would have him controlled lest he use the lass for a shield as he mounts the deck."

"That would be wise. I think you'd suffice well in the guise of smuggler. Should such ever be your desire, 'twould be the pleasure of my brother and myself to see to your training in the art."

Marcus chuckled at the suggestion. "A fair offer to the man who holds pistol to your head, Rolfe."

Rolfe turned to face him. "You are a fair man, my lord. Never has it been said that a Rolfe denied a man his due. I think 'tis the better of the deal my brother and myself would be getting should we have such as you as apprentice."

Penelope heard the tred on the steps as the crewman came below deck. Her throat constricted at the sound. Then the rap came on the cabin door.

"My lord," came the call. "My lord."

The snoring ceased. A grunt of displeasure came from the darkness. "What is it?" the baron demanded, his tone belligerent.

" 'Tis your presence the captain would have above deck. 'Tis of the utmost importance."

"What is it? You have invaded my sleep."

"I know not, my lord. 'Twas by his order I came for you."

"Oh, very well. Tell him I shall attend him momentarily."

Penelope held her breath as the sounds of his movements in the darkness filled the cabin. Then a sliver of light appeared as the hatch was opened and he stepped through. She gave a word of thanks when the door again closed without his taking notice of her.

With many exclamations of irritation, the baron made his way up the steps to the main deck of the ship. He had barely gained the deck when the pistol came to bear against his head.

"Control what enters your mind, Prussian fool,"

Marcus said, "lest I complete the job begun earlier on the dueling ground."

The baron froze in position. "Englishman?" he asked finally.

"None other. Now, come. Step forward to the main mast. Make haste, lest the flint find its way from under my touch and you discover the feel of ball in flesh."

His steps hesitant, the baron moved toward the center of the main deck. "I shall have your life for this," he muttered as he neared the mainmast.

" 'Tis an echo from days ago that I hear. Tempt me not, beast, lest I forget the promise I have made and do away with you this moment."

"Promise? What promise is it you speak of?"

Marcus laughed heartily as they came to the mainmast. "Ah, 'tis your fate of which I speak, noble Prussian. Turn with your back to the mast."

Moments later, at Marcus's command, the seaman had lashed the Prussian to the mast. The baron, his eyes bulging, his features flushed with the blood of anger, rasped, "You shall know the weight of my wrath for this, you English fool."

"Rave on, fat one," Marcus said, turning to the stairs leading below decks. Over his shoulder, he called, "There is no need for the pistol to remain at your head, Rolfe. Remind yourself, however, that 'tis still in my possession."

"Have no fear," Rolfe called from the wheel. "We've struck a bargain. 'Twill not be I who breaks it."

Making his way down the stairs to the cabin, Marcus rapped lightly on the door. When no answer came to his summons, he pushed the door inward and stepped inside.

All was darkness when he entered the cabin. He stood for a moment with the open door behind him before saying, "Penny?"

Silence followed the statement for the space of several heartbeats. Then the loud exhalation of her breath filled the cabin with sound. "Oh, Marcus!" she cried. "Is it really you? Am I indeed saved from the fate which seemed so certain but minutes ago?"

He chuckled in relief at hearing her voice. "Where are you, lass? This blasted darkness does defy my eyes in their search for you."

"Here," she called, sobs of relief stilting her words. "Ah, my Marcus. That you could imagine the thoughts I've had for you in the last hours."

Nearing her, he knelt and pulled her to him. " 'Tis over, lass," he said, holding her close. "Come, to your feet. We shall go to the main deck and away from this ship."

"My hands," she got out, reluctant to have him release his hold on her.

His touch went down her arms to the bonds which held her. The next moment she felt the blade of a knife slide against her skin, and suddenly the needles of freedom's pain swept through her wrists. Then his hands were on her arms, lifting her to her feet to lead her from the cabin.

The night air struck her as she gained the main deck. Relief at her salvation sung along her nerves, removing the sense of pain left by the bonds and the rough usage of Von Lentin. Then she came to a halt, her breath drawn, her hands coming up to point at the obese man tied to the main mast.

"Easy, lass," Marcus soothed her. "There's nothing he can do now."

Regaining her composure, she stepped firmly forward until she was within a foot of the vile baron who had been responsible for her distress. "I would have him dead, Marcus," she said bitterly. Then she soundly slapped the face of the Prussian.

"Penny," Marcus whispered. " 'Tis not for you nor I to deal with the man. Come. The longboat awaits."

She turned, fire coming to her eyes. "Marcus, is it in your mind to allow him his freedom? There shall be little rest for any of us if he remains alive. Do you think he ceases his thinking toward doing you or the Rothschilds ill?"

"No. There is no such thought in my head. 'Twill be seen to, lass. Concern yourself not. Now bid the Prussian offal farewell and let us go to the long boat. Your father and brother will be much relieved to know of your safety."

At the mention of her family, her expression changed. Returning her attention to the baron, she stood for a long moment before saying, "You are indeed a toad of monstrous proportions. Would that Marcus had done for you in the duel."

The Prussian's eyes were on Marcus. " 'Tis your day, Englishman," he muttered. "But count yourself fortunate. 'Tis not the last you have heard of Baron Von Lentin."

The threat brought a loud guffaw from the ship's captain. "And is it a fish you are, coarse-voiced Prussian? For it is surely such you shall need be to survive the journey you are about to take."

"Enough," Marcus snapped. "Such is not for the ears of the lass." Taking her arm, he turned her toward the side of the ship. "To the longboat with you, Penny."

"Your duke intends that I shall die," the Prussian called, his voice breaking. "He intends to murder me."

"No, Prussian," Marcus answered. " 'Tis but just payment of a debt overdue which is to take place. Farewell."

Without warning, the baron's voice came in a whine. "My Lady Rothschild, I beg of you. Do not allow him to do such a thing. I will return to my country, never to bother you again should I be spared."

The plea stopped her in her tracks. She turned,

studying his face in the moonlight. Suddenly her shoulders sagged and she turned to Marcus. "Ah, 'tis a fool I am, Marcus. Is it not . . ."

"Into the longboat with you, lass," he ordered. "The business at hand is as it should be. I will brook no argument from any on the matter. 'Tis unbecoming the station of a duchess to intrude into such decisions."

Her exhaustion of the ordeal just past allowed only the order to penetrate her thoughts. With a nod, she made her way to the boat and seated herself. Then the tears came and she sobbed into clenched fists as Marcus applied his weight to the oars.

An officer of the crown awaited their arrival at the dock. Immediately he asked, "My lord Duke, where would this Prussian of whom I am told be found?"

Marcus assisted Penelope to the dock and turned to point at the shadow of the ship which was already making its way out to sea. "He is aboard that ship, sir."

Anxiety was on the face of the officer as his eyes found the ship. "And whose ship is that, my lord? 'Tis the entire group of these villains I would have."

"I know not," Marcus lied. "I am but satisfied that the Lady Rothschild is safe. There is naught else concerns me." He turned back to Penelope. "Come, my lady. 'Tis rest you need. Let us to Rothschild Halls."

"But my lord Duke," the officer protested. "I shall—"

"Allow me to return the lady to her concerned family," Marcus finished for him, "lest your superiors hear of the weight you add to her cares."

With a glance through the darkness at the ship, the officer sighed. "It is my feeling you do not wish the perpetrator of this crime to come into my hands. So be it, sir." He smiled faintly. "I sense you have no concern as to the punishment of the Prussian."

Marcus returned the smile. "My only concern is for the lady. Justice shall fall on those who are deserving of such, my word on that." Taking Penelope's arm, he guided her through the group of onlookers to the inn.

"Ah, well done, sir," the innkeeper said on seeing Marcus. "And it would seem the boat of the Collingston lad was all he claimed."

"Aye, that and more. And when that lad returns, tell him that he is to call at Barrington when he will. 'Tis the business of design the boy should be involved in. He has earned as much this night."

The innkeeper's eyes widened in appreciation. "Aye, 'tis a noble thing you do for him, my lord. I wager his dreams have come true this night."

"Enough. I would have a carriage for the lady and myself."

"Immediately," was the answer.

CHAPTER SEVENTEEN

Upon their arrival at Rothschild Halls in the early morning light, Marcus reached to touch the girl lightly. "Penny," he called, "we're home. Even now your father and those who love you come. Awaken."

Her eyelids fluttered, then she came fully awake. As she sat up, her hands went to her face and then to her hair. "Oh, 'tis a sight I must be, Marcus," she moaned. "I would not have any see me in such straits."

Her words brought a laugh from him. "Think you your loved ones concern themselves with your appearance, lass? 'Tis your safety they—" He broke off as the carriage door was jerked open by Charles.

"Ah, Pen," the young man said, relief heavy in his voice. "The blessings of a great God have been showered on the Rothschilds. Come, allow me to assist you."

"Daughter," the earl sighed, tears filling his eyes. "Oh, that you could know the concern we've held for you. 'Tis . . ."

She came from the carriage to the arms of her father, tears of happiness flowing down her cheeks. " 'Tis happy I am once again to see the halls," she said amidst her sobbing.

"Come," Charles said. "We would have the tale of what has passed."

A happy Becky came running from the halls at that moment. "Oh, my lady. I'd thought you gone forever from my sight." Then she, too, broke into tears.

"And what of the Prussian?" the earl asked as Penelope pulled away from him to embrace her brother and the abigail.

"The matter is seen to," Marcus assured him. "There shall be nothing to fear from that quarter."

Penelope released her hold on Charles to say, "Aye, Father. 'Tis a fool I am, though. There was a moment when, had Marcus not . . ." She stopped, her breath indrawn. Swinging around, she faced Marcus. "I . . . I . . ."

"Yes, my lady?" Marcus asked, a smile coming to his face.

She shook her head as if to clear it. "My memory does play tricks. 'Tis not possible I should have overlooked such a thing."

"What is it, my daughter?" Rothschild asked, stepping to her. "What concerns you?"

"'Tis nothing, Father," she answered sadly, tearing her eyes from Marcus. "'Twas only a dream I had during the coach ride to the halls. I feel the need of rest."

"Aye," Marcus said. "You shall need much rest should your decision be as I wish it, for the voyage to America will try even the strength of a duchess such as you."

She'd taken two steps toward the house when his words caught her. She stopped instantly and for a long moment stood as a statue. Then, with a cry of happiness, she spun and ran into his waiting arms. "Ah, my love," she murmured amidst new tears. "Is it true? Do my ears deceive me? Am I truly to be . . ."

"Mine for evermore," he told her as his lips settled on hers.

"Ahem," the earl coughed. " 'Tis many things I'm sure we should be about. Come, all of you. It seems our Penelope has received that which she requires to recover from her ordeal."

The two were still in a tight embrace when Charles stood aside to allow Becky to enter the house before him. He sent one backward glance toward the couple and smiled before stepping across the threshold. " 'Tis a woman my sister has become of a sudden," he told his father.

"Aye, and a happy one," the earl answered.

Dell's Delightful
Candlelight Romances

☐ **THE CAPTIVE BRIDE**
   by Lucy Phillips Stewart **$1.50**   (17768-5)

☐ **FORBIDDEN YEARNINGS**
   by Candice Arkham **$1.25**   (12736-X)

☐ **A HEART TOO PROUD**
   by Laura London **$1.50**   (13498-6)

☐ **HOLD ME FOREVER** by Melissa Blakely **$1.25**   (13488-9)

☐ **THE HUNGRY HEART** by Arlene Hale **$1.25**   (13798-5)

☐ **LOVE IS THE ANSWER**
   by Louise Bergstrom **$1.25**   (12058-6)

☐ **LOVE'S SURPRISE** by Gail Everett .... **95¢**   (14928-2)

☐ **LOVE'S UNTOLD SECRET**
   by Betty Hale Hyatt **$1.25**   (14986-X)

☐ **NURSE IN RESIDENCE** by Arlene Hale ...... **95¢**   (16620-9)

☐ **ONE LOVE FOREVER**
   by Meredith Babeaux Brucker **$1.25**   (19302-8)

☐ **PRECIOUS MOMENTS**
   by Suzanne Roberts **$1.25**   (19621-3)

☐ **THE RAVEN SISTERS** by Dorothy Mack **$1.25**   (17255-1)

☐ **THE SUBSTITUTE BRIDE**
   by Dorothy Mack **$1.25**   (18375-8)

☐ **TENDER LONGINGS** by Barbara Lynn **$1.25**   (14001-3)

☐ **UNEXPECTED HOLIDAY**
   by Libby Mansfield **$1.50**   (19208-0)

☐ **WHEN DREAMS COME TRUE**
   by Arlene Hale .... **95¢**   (19461-X)

☐ **WHEN SUMMER ENDS** by Gail Everett .... **95¢**   (19646-9)

Dell Bestsellers